A Slice of Bacon?

Longarm grabbed his .45 and tumbled off the cot to the floor, banging his knee when he did so. He scrambled up and charged forward. Threw the flimsy canvas partition aside and found himself facing a swarthy man holding a knife.

The fellow was skinny and unshaven. His knife was long and slightly curved. The polished blade gleamed in the thin light coming over the partitions from a string of lanterns in the corridor beyond.

Bethlehem Bacon lay cowering on her cot, the intruder standing over her with his blade poised above her torso.

"Do it, mister, an' you die," Longarm said, straightening to his full height and cocking the Colt in his hand . . .

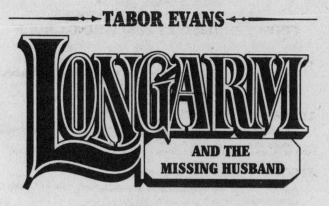

→→ TABOR EVANS ←←

LONGARM

AND THE MISSING HUSBAND

JOVE BOOKS, NEW YORK

BERKLEY PUBLISHING GROUP
Published by the Penguin Group
Penguin Group (USA) LLC
375 Hudson Street, New York, New York 10014

USA • Canada • UK • Ireland • Australia • New Zealand • India • South Africa • China

penguin.com

A Penguin Random House Company

LONGARM AND THE MISSING HUSBAND

A Jove Book / published by arrangement with the author

For information, address: The Berkley Publishing Group,
a division of Penguin Group (USA) LLC,
375 Hudson Street, New York, New York 10014.

ISBN: 978-0-515-15552-5

PUBLISHING HISTORY
Jove mass-market edition / February 2015

PRINTED IN THE UNITED STATES OF AMERICA

10 9 8 7 6 5 4 3 2 1

Cover illustration by Milo Sinovcic.

Chapter 1

Longarm awoke slowly, luxuriating under the covers with his eyes closed. Until he opened his eyes and saw that there was daylight outside the window. Unless he moved his butt, he would be late for work. Again.

He pushed the covers back and, yawning, sat up on the side of the bed for a moment. He rubbed his eyes—he'd had a very late night—and yawned again.

A hand passed over his cheeks confirmed what he already knew. He needed a shave. That would just have to wait, however. At this hour every barbershop in Denver would be as stuffed as a Christmas goose. Besides, the felons he was likely to apprehend would not much care whether the arresting deputy U.S. marshal needed a shave or not.

There seemed nothing for it except to get up and go to the office. He yawned again and shuddered as a chill ran down his spine. What he really needed was a cup of coffee. Or, he thought with a smile, a shot or two of Maryland distilled rye whiskey. Either of those could set a man up for the day.

In the meantime . . . He stood and stretched, smoothed his mustache, and ran a hand over unruly hair, then reached for his balbriggans and stepped into them. Picked up his shirt and trousers from the chair where he had draped them sometime before dawn and put those on. Pulled on his socks and slipped his feet into his stovepipe cavalry boots but refrained from stamping his feet into them. Stuffed his string tie into a pocket. Finally reached for his brown tweed coat and snuff brown flat-crowned Stetson.

"Where you goin', sweetheart?" a small voice came from beneath the bedcovers.

"Work, darlin'. I got to go," Longarm replied.

"But, Custis, aren't you gonna fuck me again? Please? I do really like a morning fuck."

"Can't do it, Angela, much as I'd like to. I got t' go to work." He grinned. "Besides, you like t' wore me out last night. Good as you are, darlin', it might could be days before my dick is rested enough t' get a hard-on again."

"Did you really like it, Custis? Was I good?" A swatch of jet-black hair and one very bright blue eyeball peeped out from beneath the covers. "Honest now."

"You were wonderful," he assured her. He buckled his gun belt around his waist, shifting it back and forth slightly until the position felt exactly right, then he leaned down, pulled the covers back a few inches, and kissed Angela. And kissed her again.

He was tempted to give in and stay for another pleasant hour or so. But he really did have to leave. Dammit.

Longarm reached beneath the covers and gave Angela's left nipple a pinch. The girl squealed. And laughed. "You come back when you can give me a proper fucking, Custis," she said.

"I will."

"Promise?"

"Promise," he assured her and turned away.

By the time he reached the door, that and all the other promises he might have made to her were forgotten. There were other things on Deputy Marshal Custis Long's mind now.

Chapter 2

Longarm skipped lightly up the stone steps leading into the Federal Building on Denver's Colfax Avenue. He was a tall man, well over six feet in height, and was a study in brown: seal brown hair and handlebar mustache, brown checked shirt, brown corduroy trousers, light brown vest, and brown tweed coat.

The brown was relieved only by the gleaming back of his boots and his gun belt. And by the black gutta-percha grips of his double-action .45 Colt revolver visible at his belly in the cross-draw holster he wore there.

He paused to hold the door for a young woman who was emerging from the building. The lady was in tears, her shoulders jerking with her repeated sobs.

"Miss?"

She stopped and looked up at him. "I'm sorry, sir. I didn't mean to get in your way."

"You ain't in my way, miss, but I can't help noticin' that something seems t' be troubling you. Maybe I can help?" Longarm said.

She shook her head. "No, I . . . I'm sure no one can help me."

Longarm was on time for a change. But this young woman . . .

She was, he guessed, in her middle twenties or thereabouts. A small woman with brown hair and golden eyes, puffy now from crying but he suspected they were very pretty when she was calm. She wore a fitted shirtwaist that showed a trim figure. About five feet tall, he guessed. And her waist was impossibly tiny.

She was pretty. If she washed the tear tracks from her face and put on a dab of rouge, she would be a beauty.

She wore a small hat pinned to the back of her head. She either had her hair pulled back in a severe bun or had it cut exceptionally short.

All in all, she was a little bit of a thing. Longarm towered over her.

"I sure can't help if you won't let me try," Longarm said gently. With a twinge of apprehension that this time he was going to be very late to the office, he said, "Whyn't you an' me go have a cup o' coffee, an' you can tell me what's troubling you," he offered. With a smile he added, "Most any burden gets lighter if there's two folks t' carry it."

"You're very kind," she said. "but really, no one can help."

"Maybe you haven't asked the right folks t' help carry whatever is burdening you, miss."

"It is missus, sir, not miss. And that is the problem. My husband is missing and no one seems able to help me find him."

Husband. Such a disappointing word, he thought. But still . . .

"Come on," he said, offering his arm and guiding her back down the steps he had just come up. "I know where we can get that coffee."

Chapter 3

The café was two blocks down and a block over. It was frequented by politicians and lawyers and other such low types. But it was the sort of place where you could buy a cup of coffee and sit at one of the tables for hours without ever being bothered or made to feel that you were not welcome.

Longarm frequently had breakfast there when he was in town and had the time, but he had never brought a woman there before. The owner, a German named Klaus, gave Longarm a questioning look when he came in with a lady on his arm.

They sat at a table in the far back corner of the place. Longarm held a chair for the woman and suggested, "There's a loo in the back. I'd imagine they would have a basin an' pitcher of water if you want t' wash some o' them tears away. Meantime I'll get us the coffee. Or would you rather have tea?"

"Coffee will be fine," she said, "and you're right, I would like to dash a little water on my face. Excuse me. I won't be long."

Longarm got up and pulled the chair out for her to rise again. When she was gone, he went to the counter. "Two coffees, please, Klaus, an' some o' them sweet crullers, too, I think."

When the lady returned, Longarm again seated her, then said, "I think maybe we should work on some introductions first thing. My name is Long. Custis Long. But my friends an' some o' my enemies, too, call me Longarm. I'm a deputy United States marshal."

The lady's eyes went wide and she sat up straighter. "A deputy. Then perhaps a very kind providence has brought me to you, Marshal Long. I am Bethlehem Bacon."

It was a good name, he thought, for she certainly looked edible to him now that the tear tracks had been wiped away.

She seemed to be waiting for something although he was not sure what. He wasted a few moments by sipping from his coffee and reaching for a cruller. It was sticky with sugar and still warm from the oven. Or oil or however it was that they made the things. That was something that was up to Klaus's wife, Berta, who presided over the kitchen in back.

"What?" Bethlehem said after a few moments. "No jokes about my name?"

"No, ma'am," Longarm said, careful of his expression. He, of course, had thought about it but was not rude enough to comment at the lady's expense. He took a bite of the cruller. It melted in his mouth.

"Please call me Beth," she said.

He smiled and said, "Try one o' these crullers. They're splendid."

She ignored the pastries but did take a drink of coffee after loading it with cream and sugar. Longarm waited for her to feel like talking.

"My husband," she said. "I think he may have been killed by wild Indians. I went to the Bureau of Indian Affairs Office. That is where I was coming from when you saw me. They said . . ." She looked like she was going to cry again. "They said there is nothing they can do."

"You didn't talk t' the marshal?" he asked.

"No. Why would I? It was on the Indian reservation where Hank disappeared. My husband was . . . he was surveying for a railroad extension through the Indian lands. Then he just . . . disappeared. One man I talked to suggested that he might have left me. Oh, he didn't come right out and say that. But he intimated it strongly enough that I certainly understood what he meant."

Beth Bacon toyed with her spoon. Turned her cup around and around. Longarm finished his cruller and reached for another. He had not taken time for breakfast this morning and the pastries were going down pretty nicely, never mind the lady's troubles.

"You're gonna have t' tell me more," Longarm said, drinking a little coffee to wash the crullers down. "Then maybe you an' me can go back over to the Fed'ral Building an' talk to my boss, see if he'll let me go have a look-see. But I got t' know everything you do about this. Then . . . no promises, but then we'll just see what we can see."

He gave Beth a reassuring smile and helped himself to the last cruller as she did not seem to be interested in it.

Chapter 4

"The man is a surveyor, boss," Longarm said, standing in front of moonfaced and balding U.S. Marshal William Vail. Vail looked like a typical bureaucrat in his boiled shirt and sleeve garters, but in fact, he was as salty as any of his deputies. In his youth, which was not that long ago, he had been a Texas Ranger and a rough old boy. Now he sent other men out to do the things he himself had done in the past.

"He's tryin' to work out the route for a railroad extension. Others will come along after him t' do the final surveys an' lay out the tracks. But now Hank Bacon is missin'. No one seems t' know where he is nor what happened to him. An' the way I figure, it bein' on reservation land makes it our affair.

"Miz Bacon has already gone to the BIA an' they don't want nothing t' do with her nor with him. 'Bout all they want is for her t' go away an' pretend nothing's wrong."

Vail leaned back in his chair and peered across his desk at the pretty lady. Who might or might not be a widow at this point. He pondered the question for a long moment, then he leaned forward with a loud creak of the springs under his chair and said, "I agree. It is within our jurisdiction."

"Does that mean I c'n go, Billy?" Longarm asked.

Vail nodded and with a grunt said, "You can go."

Beth Bacon squealed with happiness. She dashed around Vail's desk and planted a wet kiss on his red cheek.

Damn, Longarm thought, wishing he was the one to get that hug and kiss of happiness.

Still, it was probably for the best that she chose Billy instead. Longarm just would have embarrassed himself with a hard-on, he acknowledged. There was just something about Mrs. Bacon that made him want to get her drawers off.

But then there was something about most women that made him respond that way. Lucky for him, women often found him attractive, too, something he could not really understand as he was more craggy and rugged than he was handsome.

He never could have been a model for one of those catalog drawings that advertised shirts or cigarettes or whatnot. Hammers, maybe, or stock saddles. But definitely nothing that required a pretty boy. Custis Long was not that and never had been, not on his best day.

He reached forward and touched Beth on the elbow to bring her attention back to him. He shot his chin in the direction of the door, and she took the hint.

"I can't thank you enough, Marshal. Thank you ever so much," she gushed.

She followed Longarm out then said, "How will we travel?"

"Travel where?" he asked, both of them standing in front of Henry's desk, Henry being Billy Vail's chief clerk.

"Why, to Wyoming Territory, of course," she said.

"Little missy," Longarm said, "*we* ain't going to Wyoming. I are. Uh, I am, that is. You are stayin' right here 'til I get back."

"Oh, but I can't stay here. For one thing, I don't have money to pay for a hotel. It took everything I had to get to

Denver in the first place. So I couldn't stay here even if I wanted to."

"Sure you can," he said. "I'll park you in my room. It ain't so much, but my landlady will be happy t' have another female on the premises for a change. We'll talk to her. See if we can work out something toward you eating at her table, too, though it ain't usually board, just room." He smiled. "Don't you worry. We'll work it out. Now you can set over there for a few minutes an' wait while Henry here comes up with my travel vouchers."

Beth did not look especially happy about the arrangement, but she dutifully went over to the side of the room and perched on one of the chairs against the wall there while Longarm conducted his business with Henry.

Chapter 5

Beth went with him to his rooming house, where she was welcomed with open arms. Welcomed to stay in his room while he was away, too. Longarm left her there and picked up his carpetbag, already packed and ready as it was at all times.

"I've arranged for you to take your meals here, too," Longarm told her. "With any kind o' luck, I won't be gone all that long anyway. I'll see what I can learn about your husband an' hopefully find him safe an' sound. Meantime, you'll be fine here."

"Thank you, Marshal." She smiled and squeezed his hand. Even that small, innocent contact made his dick hard. There was something powerfully attractive about Bethlehem Bacon, something he could not put a name to but could certainly feel.

Longarm thought about taking his saddle and rifle along but settled for just the bag. The rest of his gear remained in his room with Beth.

When he left for the train station, he had an impulse to lean down and kiss her but he refrained from doing it. Even so, he was a good five blocks away in a hansom cab before his hard-on completely subsided and he could put his mind to business.

"Which station will you be wanting, sir?" the hack driver called down to him.

"Wynkoop," Longarm responded. The depot at Wazee and Wynkoop was the oldest in town and the closest to the rooming house. Longarm smiled a little to himself. The driver was undoubtedly hoping he would want the station where the Denver to Cheyenne line intersected with the Kansas Pacific line. That newer depot was farther north and would have resulted in a larger fare. Longarm was traveling on the taxpayers' dollars, but that did not mean he could be wasteful.

He settled back in the seat of the hack and wondered just how in the hell he was supposed to find Hank Bacon when he got to the White River Indian Reservation.

He tugged his hat low over his eyes and attempted to doze on the drive to the railway station. After all, he had gotten practically no sleep the night before.

Not that he regretted the evening. It had not been time wasted. Far from it.

What *was* it about Beth Bacon, though, that made her so damned desirable?

He had had Angela for hours on end last night, had her in nearly every way a man could think of, yet now it was Beth on whom his thoughts lay. It was a puzzlement.

Chapter 6

Longarm spent the trip up to Cheyenne in the smoking car playing cards with some friendly travelers, one a priest whose luck—if it was luck—was phenomenal. The man won and won and won some more. If he had stayed in the game much longer, Longarm figured he would have gone broke before they reached Fort Collins. Fortunately the priest took his winnings, and his Bible, and left the game after an hour or so. After that Longarm was able to get back at least a little of what he had lost to the man with the turned-around collar.

They reached Cheyenne in the middle of the night. A conductor came through warning everyone, and waking them, ten minutes or so out.

"If you leave anything behind, make sure it's something valuable. I'll give it to my old lady for an anniversary present," the man said. Longarm was not sure if he meant that or not. Not that Longarm had so very much baggage to keep track of. There was just his carpetbag and he had that with him in the smoking car.

When the train lurched to a clattering, clanking halt at the Cheyenne station, Longarm got up from the table where he had been playing and thanked the other gents for the pleasure of the game.

"Next time let us win a little, Long," a drummer dealing in yard goods said.

Longarm grinned. "Next time bring more money with you, Horace."

Longarm retrieved his carpetbag from the overhead rack where he had left it and followed the crowd out of the car onto the platform at Cheyenne. The night air felt chilly after the smoky confinement of the railroad coach. He turned his collar up and headed for the Union Pacific depot nearby.

When he got there . . .

"What the hell are you doing here, dammit? I thought I left you safe an' sound back in Denver," he bawled.

Bethlehem Bacon smiled at him as if he had just paid her a friendly compliment. "It is nice to see you, too, Marshal."

"But . . ."

"I know. You were trying to protect me. But I couldn't abide staying there, always waiting, never knowing what was happening up here. So"—she spread her hands and smiled so very sweetly again—"so here I am."

"How? I mean . . . I thought you said you were broke. How'd you get a ticket?"

"That was simple enough," the lady said. "I told them I was traveling with you. They charged my fare to the government or somebody. Anyway here I am."

"Yes, here you are," Longarm said. "The question now is, what the hell am I gonna do with you here in Cheyenne? I don't have anyplace up here where I can dump you while I try an' find your husband."

"Exactly," Beth said. "So I shall go with you." She smiled just about the sweetest, prettiest smile he had ever seen. "Now," she said as if that silliness were all settled, "let's go find out when the next westbound train will be coming through."

Chapter 7

"We should get off at Rawlins," Beth told him after they were established in one of the passenger coaches—*not* a smoking car—and on their way. Longarm simply had not known what else to do with the sneaky female and so brought her along with him. "But only until I can figure out where t' put you for a spell," he had agreed.

"An' why Rawlins 'stead of Rock Springs? That'd be closer to where you said he disappeared," he told Beth now after her pronouncement.

"Because Rawlins is where Hank's employers have an office. You'll want to speak with them before you go looking for him," she said, sounding very sure of herself.

"Why didn't you tell me that before?" he said.

"You didn't ask. Oh, here comes the butcher boy. Buy me a doughnut, will you?"

Longarm was well aware that Beth had just changed the subject. But he really did not know what to do with her. He bought her the doughnut. And one for himself although he would rather have had a cigar and a shot of rye.

The Union Pacific westbound reached Rawlins late in the morning. With a sigh, Longarm and Beth Bacon left the train there.

"You don't have any luggage with you?" he asked, retrieving his much-traveled carpetbag from the overhead rack.

"Just this handbag," she said. For a handbag it was large but it was no suitcase. He wondered just how much she could be carrying in there.

Longarm helped Beth down onto the platform and led the way to the Elkhorn Hotel. He had stayed there before and knew it was not fancy, but it was clean and accommodating, with a café next door where you could get exceptional rhubarb pie.

"Hello, Marshal. Two rooms for you?" the clerk said and with a rather oily smile added, "Adjoining?"

Longarm looked down at Beth, who was acting innocent as a child. She had no money to pay for a room. He knew that. He also knew that Henry would not approve payment for two rooms for one deputy. "One room," he said.

The clerk's eyebrows rose but the man said nothing, just turned the register book around for Longarm to sign.

Beth said nothing either. If anything, she acted like it was the most normal thing in the world for her to share a room with a man who was not her husband.

Longarm accepted the room key and led the way upstairs to room number four. Beth meekly followed him inside and perched on the side of the bed while Longarm deposited his carpetbag inside the mahogany wardrobe.

"We can have a cot brought in," Beth said firmly. "I will sleep there."

"Got this all figured out, do you?"

"All? No. But enough for the time being."

"What about meals? D'you expect the government t' pay for those for you?"

"The government does not have to know." She giggled. "You will just run into very expensive dining. Anyway, most of the time we will be beyond restaurants and such civilization. You will buy trail foods at government expense. I support the government by way of taxes. It seems only fair that the government support me for a few days in return."

"Like I said before, you got this all figured out." He sighed. Longarm felt like he was finding himself sighing quite a bit of late. He poured a little water into the basin and washed his hands and face then said, "All right, are you ready t' go see your husband's bosses?"

"Can we eat first?" Beth asked. "I'm hungry."

Longarm sighed again.

Chapter 8

Longarm could say one thing for the girl. She had an appetite. He didn't think he had ever seen anyone so small put away so much food. She ate like there was no tomorrow.

But then, come to think of it, perhaps she really felt that tomorrow was in doubt.

She was far from home with no money, depending on a stranger to help her get by, help that as far as she knew could be withdrawn at any moment.

So perhaps it was no surprise that Bethlehem Bacon was packing away as much as she could as fast as she could manage.

Longarm let her fill herself while he sat back and had a light meal, then drank coffee until Beth ran out of room.

"Satisfied?" he asked. And pretended not to notice that she filched a pair of yeast rolls and hid them in a pocket of her dress.

"Yes, I am, thank you."

"Can we go see Hank's boss now?" Longarm said.

"Of course. That's why we are here, after all." Acting very prim and proper, Beth led the way to a suite of second-floor offices of the Berriman and Jones Land and Investments Co. Inc.

Interesting title, Longarm thought. It would cover almost anything Messrs. Berriman and Jones wanted to undertake.

"Have you been here before?" Longarm asked on their way up the stairs.

Beth shook her head. "No, but Hank told me about it. To tell you the truth, he wasn't sure about the partners, but they offered him a very generous salary."

Longarm raised an eyebrow at that information.

"I have no idea what happened to his pay," Beth said, "or if he even got any. He never sent anything back home. He wrote to me, of course, but he never sent any money. I kind of think he didn't get any, but I don't know that for sure."

"We'll ask his bosses about that. If they are holding his pay for some reason, maybe they will hand it over to you."

"It would be nice to have something other than my night-shirt and some tooth powder in my handbag," she said.

Longarm opened the door for Beth to enter the Berriman and Jones office. There was no receptionist in the small inner office. A door leading into a larger office in the back stood open. A man in sleeve garters and an eyeshade was seated at a rolltop desk there. He looked up when Longarm and Beth came in.

Rising, the man came into the reception area. He was tall and slender, bald but with wildly bushy eyebrows and a very thin, graying mustache. "May I help you?"

"Are you one o' the partners?" Longarm asked before Beth could launch into her tale of woe.

"I am, sir. I am Honus Berriman. And you are . . ."

"I am Mrs. Bethlehem Bacon, and I want to know where my husband is," Beth blurted out in a rush.

"Ah, yes. Mrs. Bacon. We received your telegrams, of course. I only wish I knew what to tell you," Berriman said. "Would you care to come in and sit while we talk?" The man smiled and spread his hands palms upward. "Not that there is so very much to talk about. You probably know everything that we do. We lost touch with your husband several weeks ago. Haven't heard a word since."

Berriman ushered them into the main office, which was larger than the reception area and held two desks, a bookcase, and two file cabinets. "Please. Sit down, Mrs. Bacon." He fetched the chair from the other desk for Beth. He ignored Longarm and did not offer to find him a chair.

"Is there anything I can do for you?" Berriman asked, not sounding like he particularly meant it.

Chapter 9

"Perhaps you know that the government grants land hold-ings on every other section along a railroad right of way. Our purpose is more the land than the railroad, although that would be nice to have, too. In order to get the land, though, we have to lay track.

"There is already another company planning to build a line north running east of the Big Horns. Our idea is to build west of that mountain range. The line would be shorter by a good many miles, and that would lessen the cost of construction," Berriman told them.

"Wouldn't that also reduce the amount of land you can get from the government?" Longarm asked.

Berriman glanced up at him as if annoyed. Longarm had not told the man what he did for a living, and Berri-man had expressed no curiosity about who Longarm was or why he should be accompanying Beth Bacon. Probably he assumed Longarm was Beth's brother or some other close relative and was acting as her chaperone.

"We have done some calculating, of course. The land grant would be more than adequate, and our construction expenses would be greatly reduced," Berriman said. "Now,

Mrs. Bacon," he said, turning his attention entirely back to Beth, "I wish I could help you, but like we told you in those telegrams, we really do not know anything.

"Your husband outfitted in Cheyenne and took a train west to Rock Springs. After that we know nothing of him or his whereabouts." Berriman said.

Beth took a deep breath and straightened in her chair. "What about Hank's pay?" she bluntly asked. The girl had sand, Longarm conceded. Maybe, he thought, smiling to himself, it was all that lunch she managed to pack away before they came to the office.

"Pardon?" Berriman said.

"I said what about the salary you promised Hank?" Beth persisted.

"We paid it to him, of course," Berriman said.

"You did not," Beth declared firmly. "Hank would have sent some of his pay home if he received any. It is obvious that you didn't pay him at all. And now he is missing. Have you done something to my husband so you won't have to pay him what you owe?"

"Madam! How can you say such a thing? An accusation . . . unfounded . . ." Berriman sputtered with anger. Tiny droplets of spittle flew off his lip, and his face, except for the tip of his nose, became red. His nose was dead white. "I will not hear . . . cannot listen . . . *really*."

Berriman dragged a kerchief from his pocket and mopped his forehead. Then he pulled his shoulders back. "I shall have to ask you to leave," he snapped and turned his chair so that his back was to Beth and Longarm.

Beth seemed inclined to stay and argue but Longarm tapped her on the shoulder and motioned for her to leave. If Honus Berriman was that offended—or pretended to be— there probably was no point in arguing with him.

"Come on," Longarm said when they were outside the Berriman and Jones offices and on their way back downstairs. "We'll go get us some coffee an' think this through."

Rye whiskey and a good cigar would have been even better, but under the circumstances, coffee would have to do.

Chapter 10

"'Bout the only thing there is t' do," Longarm said, "will be t' go to Rock Springs an' see can we run Hank down from there."

"That was my conclusion, too," Beth said over her untouched cup of coffee. Damn, Longarm thought, but she was pretty. Somehow all the more appealing by being in trouble and needing his help.

Beneath the table he got a raging hard-on just from looking at that lovely face. It was a good thing, he thought, that the table was not glass. He would not want her to see that reaction.

"It's a little late in the day now t' be heading west again. We'll get us a good night's sleep an' head out again come morning," he said.

In truth, they probably could have caught one of the UP's westbound passenger trains, or if not that, with his credentials, Longarm could have hitched a ride in the caboose of a freight train. The problem with either of those was that Beth looked dead tired now. He guessed she had not slept in days, probably not since she concluded that her husband was missing.

"We'll just relax the rest o' the afternoon," he said,

"have a nice meal, an' then turn in early. Why don't you take a nap before dinner, ma'am? I'll come wake you when it's time to eat."

"What will you do, Marshal?"

"There's some errands I want t' run," he said. "One o' them is to check the train schedule an' see what we can expect come morning."

"I . . . All right," she said. "A short nap doesn't sound bad."

Longarm paid for their coffee—hers had not been touched—and walked with her back to the hotel. He collected the room key from the clerk and went upstairs with her, saw her safely into the room, but then touched the brim of his Stetson and pulled the door closed.

Longarm went back downstairs, the room key still in his pocket, and walked out onto the streets of Rawlins.

Chapter 11

He had not reached the bottom of the stairs before he was reaching for a cheroot, had not reached the sidewalk before he got out a match to light it. And he would gladly have gulped down a slug of whiskey if only he'd had a flask with him. As it was, the whiskey had to wait for a few minutes.

He did take care of business before pleasure, though. He immediately headed for the UP depot to check the board for departures. There would be a westbound passenger train coming through at nine twenty the next morning. That should do nicely, Longarm thought.

As soon as he saw that, he turned on his heel and made a beeline for the Higgins and Co., Inc., Gentlemen's Club. He had been there before and knew it to be a pleasant place where a man could find a drink of whiskey and a game of cards without being bothered by whores cadging drinks or dealers who made their money by cheating.

The games at Higgins's were honest and the whiskey was of high quality, a splendid combination in Longarm's opinion.

Stepping inside was like finding an oasis of calm in a hectic world. The place was dark and quiet, sound muted by the sawdust spread liberally on the floor. It smelled of beer and cedar.

At this hour—too early for the serious gamblers—there were no tables in play, and only two men other than the bartender stood at the bar.

Longarm approached the bar with a sigh. Pretty as she was, it was frustrating being with Bethlehem Bacon knowing she was off limits. It was better being in his own sort of environment.

"Rye whiskey," Longarm ordered when the bartender came to him, "an' a deck o' cards still fresh in the wrapper. Make that a bottle o' rye."

"Coming right up."

An hour later the level of excellent rye in the bottle had gone down a couple inches and Longarm was on his third cheroot since leaving Beth at the hotel.

The pair of drinkers at the bar had gone but they were replaced by a trio of men in suits and ties, one of them Honus Berriman. Berriman either did not recognize Longarm . . . or chose not to. In any case, he did not acknowledge the tall deputy seated alone at a table near the back of the room.

The three took seats at a table closer to the door and were served a bottle of something without the bartender having to ask what they wanted. They began playing poker.

Longarm would have liked to join them, but it seemed clear enough that this was a private game. He doubted that he would be welcome to play with them, so dealing solitaire would have to do.

He sighed—damn, he was doing that a lot lately, ever since he'd hooked up with Beth Bacon—and began shuffling his cards preparatory to laying out yet another game.

Then the front door opened, and two men with bandanas pulled over their faces walked in.

Chapter 12

It took no great psychic powers to see what they were up to. Each carried a sawed-off double barrel. Each immediately eared back the hammers on their scatterguns.

By the time their muzzles began to lift, Longarm had his .45 in hand.

"Don't even think about it," he barked in a loud, authoritative voice.

The two robbers apparently had not seen him sitting toward the back of the room. Now his command threw them off their game for a second or two.

Both stopped moving and stared toward Longarm.

"Set those guns down nice an' easy," Longarm commanded. "Don't drop 'em and don't pull the triggers."

For a moment he thought it was working. The man on his left paused, but the one on the right raised the muzzle of his shotgun and pointed it toward Berriman and his friends at the poker table.

Longarm's shot and the killer's—the two came in acting like robbers but made no demands for money, and there was very little on the poker table that would have been worth stealing—came at almost the same moment.

Honus Berriman was blown over backward, his chair

clattering to the floor along with what remained of Berriman's face.

Longarm's 255 grain lead slug slammed into the breastbone of the shooter, spilling him onto the sawdust-littered floor.

When his partner dropped, the first man woke up from his reaction to Longarm's presence. He swung the twin barrels of his 12 gauge toward the tall lawman.

Longarm did not hesitate. His second bullet took the shotgunner low in the belly and doubled him over.

The man lost all interest in his shotgun and whatever mission had brought him into the saloon. He dropped his gun muzzle down. The jolt of striking the floor was enough to dislodge the hammer sears, and one barrel fired. The recoil drove the shotgun out of the man's hands, but by then he really did not seem to care. By then he was clutching his gut and keeling over.

The man dropped to his knees and then sprawled face forward into the sawdust with its load of mud and spit and tobacco juice.

The bartender and Berriman's two friends rushed to help him but half the man's head had been blown away by the killer. There was nothing they or anyone could do to help.

Longarm fought his way through the fog of acrid gun smoke to make sure both killers were dead, then went back to his poker table and began reloading his Colt, reminding himself that he needed to clean and oil it when he got back to the hotel.

Chapter 13

A squat, burly man with more chest and arm hair than some bears very cautiously came inside. He wore a tin star displayed on his coat and held a double-barrel shotgun.

Longarm grunted, thinking that shotguns were an awfully popular item in Rawlins this year.

"Who . . ." the town marshal began.

"Over here," Longarm volunteered.

"You killed both these men?" the marshal said, his voice gruff and demanding.

Longarm gave the man a long, slow look before he answered. "Yeah. I did."

"You are under arrest," the marshal said, not sounding quite so authoritative this time.

"Check your facts before you decide that," Longarm suggested, just as polite as he knew how. Which at the moment was not terribly polite. He did not much care for this marshal nor the man's attitude.

"Are you going to give me trouble?" the marshal said. He seemed a mite nervous when he said it.

Longarm raised a boot to the seat of the chair opposite his at the table and shoved, sending the chair out away from the table. "Set," he said firmly. "An' find out what's happened before you go arrestin' anybody."

"I can see that three men are dead here," the marshal said.

"Yes, an' I killed two of 'em," Longarm told him.

One of the men at the poker table turned away from his friend's body and said, "Leave him alone, Jonathon. He likely kept Sam and me from being shot down same as Honus was."

"They were just robbers, right?" Jonathon said.

The well-dressed gambler shook his head. "They weren't here to rob anybody, Jonathon. They came here to kill. Honus and likely Sam and me, too. This gentleman saved our bacon."

"Oh. Well." Jonathon seemed not to know what he should do next since there was no one who needed to be arrested.

"Any idea who these two were or why they would've been wanting to kill you?" Longarm asked.

"No. Of course not."

Longarm did not believe the man for a moment, but whatever the reason, he did not want to trot it out in public. "All right, suit yourself."

The gent hesitated then extended his hand. "I'm being ungrateful, aren't I? After all, you just saved our lives. My name is Cletus Berriman. This is Samuel Bannerman Jones."

"Sam," Jones put in. He had left the side of his friend's body and come to stand with his partner.

"May we buy you a drink? A meal? What can we do for you, Mr.—um? Anything, just name it."

"Long," Longarm said, taking the hint and the man's hand. "Custis Long."

"Believe me, it is our pleasure to make your acquaintance, Mr. Long."

"It's Marshal Long, actually," he said, cutting his eyes toward the stocky town badge carrier. "Deputy United States marshal out o' Denver."

"Oh, well, I . . ." The town marshal seemed both surprised and a little unnerved by that news. "I, uh . . ."

"Does that arrest order still stand?" Longarm asked bluntly.

"No, uh, of course not."

"Then get the fuck away from me before I put you under arrest for interferin' with a Fed'ral investigation."

"I . . . I . . ." Jonathon sputtered a little but turned tail and began loudly issuing wholly unnecessary orders about what should be done with the bodies.

"You're here on business?" Sam Jones said.

"Yes, sir," Longarm said, "an' if that offer of 'anything you can do' still stands, there in fact is somethin' you can do t' help."

"Name it, Marshal, up to my firstborn, and you shall have it."

Chapter 14

"I know this is a bad time t' be talking business, your partner just having been killed an' all, but there is something I need, and you boys might be able t' provide it."

"Like I said, Marshal, just name it," Jones said. Berriman, understandably, was focusing his attention on the body of his dead . . . whatever Honus had been to him, brother or cousin, uncle or, for all Longarm knew, grandfather.

"I'm here looking for a fella that seems to've gone missing. He was working for you at the time. Man name of Hank Bacon," Longarm said.

Jones took Longarm by the elbow and drew him away from the crowd that had gathered around the dead. "Can we sit over here? I have to admit that I'm a little shaky. I'm not much accustomed to violence."

Longarm went with Jones to the table where he had been playing solitaire. He pushed aside the cards he dealt minutes earlier and motioned to the bartender for another glass to go with his bottle of rye whiskey.

"Not bad," Jones said after he took a healthy slug of Longarm's rye. "I generally drink Scotch but this is nice."

Longarm had a swallow and said, "About Hank Bacon?"

"Yes. Hank. We did, in fact, hire the gentleman. He

seemed to know what he was doing even though he was
not familiar with the country out here. Neither, for that
matter, are we. We, the Berrimans and I, came out from
Pennsylvania. Going to make our fortunes, don't you see.

"The way it was told to us, there was gold . . . or at least
golden opportunity . . . practically lying in the streets,
waiting to be picked up by smart operators such as ourselves." Jones shuddered and finished his whiskey. Longarm poured him another.

"You Western boys play rough, we quickly discovered.
We should have been secretive about what we planned, but
we simply did not know that would have been a good
idea. We practically announced our intentions to the world.
That would be to attract investors to build the railroad.
We would relinquish ownership to them once it was con-
structed. What we wanted were the land grants along the
right of way. We could sell them to farmers from the East
who want in on the opportunities to be found out here.

"We thought it was a solid business plan. And the first
step was for us to determine exactly where that right of
way should be. That is why we hired Bacon."

"Why him?" Longarm asked.

"He was recommended to us by a man back home.
Hank had done some surveying for him. He said Hank was
honest and good at his job. So we hired him, outfitted him,
sent him on his way.

"For several weeks we received the occasional report
back from him. Then . . . nothing. We haven't heard from
him in some time."

"Did you know that much of any right of way west of
the Big Horns would cross reservation lands belonging
to the Shoshone and Arapaho? Those lands are not subject
to sale or grant," Longarm said. "They are already pledged to
the tribes in perpetuity."

"No, I . . . I didn't know that," Jones said.

Longarm finished his glass of rye and poured another

for Jones and then for himself. "Smoke?" he offered, pulling a cheroot out and nipping the twist off with his teeth.

"No, thanks."

Longarm took his time lighting the cheroot then leaned back in his chair. "Bad things can happen to a man traveling alone in this country," he said. "But bad things can happen right here, too."

He nodded toward the mess that the bartender was cleaning up now that the bodies had been carried off somewhere. "Like that. D'you have any enemies? You or the Berrimans, either personal or professional?"

Jones shook his head. "None that I know of. Why do you ask?"

"'Cause that was no robbery gone wrong," Longarm said. "That was a deliberate attempt at murder, an' I don't care what the penny dreadfuls say, we don't just go shooting people down out here. There was a reason those fellas came in trying to kill you three."

"You think they were after all of us?" Jones sounded nervous when he asked the question.

"If it was just Berriman that was wanted dead, there wouldn't have been two of them. Two men with shotguns at close range, I'd say somebody wants all three o' you dead."

Jones turned pale. "Dear God!"

"Think about that. Then how's about you and me have dinner tonight," Longarm said. "I'll have someone with me. Hank Bacon's wife. Or widow, as the case may be."

Longarm stood and stuck his cheroot between his teeth.

"'Bout seven o'clock? You pick the place. Come by the Elkhorn an' collect us when you're ready. Bring Clete with you if he's feeling up to it. We'll talk some more then."

Longarm touched the brim of his Stetson and headed back to the hotel to see if Beth was awake from her nap yet.

Chapter 15

Sam Jones was already in the lobby when Longarm and Beth came downstairs for supper. Longarm performed the introductions.

"Please forgive Clete for not joining us," Jones said. "After seeing his brother murdered this afternoon, he just wasn't up to going out tonight." Jones turned his attention to Longarm. "Honus's body will be prepared tonight, then Clete will take it home on the morning eastbound train. He should be away for several weeks, perhaps longer. In fact, we are tempted to abandon our Western enterprise altogether and turn our attention back to Pennsylvania."

"But what about my husband?" Beth put in. "If you just up and leave, that will abandon Hank, too."

"I wish I could tell you what has happened to Bacon," Jones said, "but I don't know. He could have run into some sort of trouble or he could simply have quit his job."

"Hank would never do that," Beth insisted.

"And you could be right about that," Jones said. "I'm sure we both hope that Marshal Long here will discover the truth, whatever it may be."

"What Marshal Long wants t' discover right now,"

Longarm said, smiling, "is a juicy steak an' a heap o' potatoes. I'm hungry an' I'm sure Mrs. Bacon is, too."

"Of course. I didn't mean to be rude. Come along then.
I know a very pleasant restaurant. We can talk business
after we eat."

Three hours later but no better informed, Longarm and
Beth returned to the Elkhorn.

"Mr. Jones seems like a very nice man," Beth conceded
on their way up to their room. "Do you think he was telling
the truth tonight?"

"He certainly seemed t' be," Longarm said.

"Even about Hank's pay?"

Longarm nodded. "I think so. A business operation the
size o' Berriman and Jones isn't likely t' worry about small
change. Which is what Hank's pay would be to them. No, I
think they paid it, just like he says they did."

"Then what could have happened to it?" she said.

"When we find out where Hank is, could be we'll know
about that, too," Longarm told her.

Beth was quiet after that, obviously thinking about
what Longarm said. And about her missing husband.

Longarm did not want to say anything more, but his sus-
picions in truth were that Hank Bacon was dead. Something
had happened to him out there. Something they might never
learn.

They reached their room, and Longarm opened the
door then let Beth enter before him.

He was not prepared for her scream.

Chapter 16

Longarm charged forward, his right hand snatching the .45 from the holster on his belt and his left shoving Beth out of the way.

His shoulder hit her in the back and sent her sprawling to the floor.

Ahead and to his right he saw a man, an intruder, in their room, who was straddling the windowsill, one leg inside the room and the other out.

"Stop, thief!" Longarm barked.

He had his Colt in hand and could easily have shot the son of a bitch, but that seemed a heavy penalty for a man to pay for a little pilfering. And, in fact, Longarm could not tell from the fellow's posture if he was just coming into the room or leaving it.

"Stop!" he shouted again.

The intruder, predictably, paid no attention to the shouted instructions. But he did eye the big .45 with considerable alarm. The black, gaping muzzle of the revolver must have looked like a cannon to him, for he went immediately pale. Stopped still as a statue.

And then threw himself sideways, out of the room, off the windowsill, and into the night.

Longarm rushed to the window and leaned out, .45 held ready, but there was no sign of the man. He had virtually disappeared, just that quickly.

There was no balcony outside the window, not even a proper ledge, and they were on the second floor. Apparently the thief had dropped to the ground and scuttled out of sight, perhaps beneath the overhang so that Longarm had no line of sight to spot him.

"Shit," Longarm muttered aloud.

"What did you say?"

He turned. For a moment he had completely forgotten Beth. She was sitting on the bedroom floor now, her hair mussed and her dress slightly askew.

"Sorry," Longarm quickly said, rushing to help her up.

He caught himself before he gave in to his automatic impulse to brush off her backside. That would not have been exactly proper.

"You said something," Beth said.

"Oh, uh, it was nothing."

"Yes you did, I heard you."

Longarm grinned. "In that case, you know what I said."

"Oh. I was right then. You did say that."

"If you say so," Longarm said. He returned to the window, leaned down, and once again looked outside, as if hoping to see someone he could shoot out there.

Reminded of the six-gun in his hand, he gave it a look as if the weapon had offended him, then he shoved the .45 back into the leather where it belonged.

"What was that all about?" Beth said.

Longarm shrugged. "Somebody tryin' to rob our room is what I'd guess. Are you all right?"

"Yes, thanks. I'm fine. Was the man just coming in or had he already had time to steal from you?" She smiled and added, "I know he didn't take anything from me. Everything I have with me is in this bag and I've had it with me all evening."

"I'll look," Longarm said.

He put his carpetbag onto the bed and rummaged through it. Things looked like they might have been disarranged, but he might have done that himself when he was shaving before they went down to dinner. If anything was taken, he did not know what it might have been.

"I guess everything's here," he said, turning.

And got his second shock of the evening.

Chapter 17

Beth was standing by the wardrobe, her back to him. She was in the process of removing her dress.

Longarm figured his eyes must have gotten as big as that thief's when he looked into the muzzle of his .45.

Beth had matter-of-factly stepped out of her dress, brushed it off a little, and hung it in the wardrobe. She had a taut, tight, rounded ass, Longarm noticed. His dick noticed, too, immediately growing hard.

Then Beth opened her oversized handbag and pulled out a nightshirt, which she proceeded to pull on over her unmentionables. Finally, reaching up underneath the nightshirt, she removed her chemise and her pantaloons.

Longarm had not exactly seen anything. But, oh, what his imagination supplied.

Only then did he notice that there was no cot in the room. Two people. One double-sized bed plenty large enough for both of them.

His dick began to throb with anticipation.

No woman would act this way in front of a man she did not intend to fuck. Surely not.

While Longarm stood there, horny as a goat, Beth went

to the washstand, poured some water into the basin, and proceeded to wash out her underthings.

Once she was done with that, she carefully draped her bits of silky clothing over the radiator.

And got into bed. Smiling.

Longarm did not intend to be found wanting. He shucked out of his clothes slick as an eel and crawled in beside her.

Chapter 18

Longarm heard a loud *crack* and suddenly saw stars and squiggles floating in front of his eyes.

"Ow, dammit," he hollered. "What'd you hit me for?"

"You're being lewd. And making some very unwelcome advances, sir. Now I suggest you get right back up and put something on. Were those balbriggans I saw you step out of? Good. Find them and put them back on."

"But you . . ."

"I have nothing in my bag but this nightshirt and my hairbrush, a few things like that. There isn't room in there for clothing, and I don't have a suitcase with me, so I shall have to wash things out as we go and brush off my dress as best I can. Finding me in this state of undress does *not*, sir, mean that I encourage your advances. I am a married lady and I intend to remain true to my husband. Is that clear, Marshal? Is that perfectly clear now?"

"Yes'm," Longarm said contritely. "Perfectly clear."

"Fine. And I shall trust you not to snore, sir, or I will poke you in the ribs. Now, please, go to sleep."

"Yes'm." Longarm crawled sheepishly out of the bed and pulled on his balbriggans, then blew out the bedside lamp, and returned to the bed.

But, oh, he was achingly aware of that pretty ass lying so close at his side and the warmth her small body gave off.

She smelled of yeast and naphtha soap and some faint, delicate perfume.

And his dick just would *not* go down.

He thought Beth had gone to sleep but after a time she stirred and said, "I understand how you men are. If you want to, well, if you want to pleasure yourself, I won't look."

It seemed a very long time before he was able to sleep.

Chapter 19

Sam Jones was in the lobby waiting for them when Longarm and Beth came down for breakfast. "Good. I'm glad I caught you before you leave to go west," Jones said.

"Has something happened?" Longarm asked. "Is anything wrong?"

"Nothing more than we already talked about," Jones said, doffing his hat and nodding toward Beth. "Clete and I talked last night. We agreed that we should give Hank's pay to Mrs. Bacon."

"I thought you said Bacon already collected his pay," Longarm said.

Jones nodded. "He did. But time moves along. And, well, we just don't know where Hank is or where we might send his next pay. So it seems only reasonable that Mrs. Bacon should have it."

Jones pulled a small change purse out of his coat pocket and handed it to Beth then said, "May I offer you two some breakfast before you leave? There won't be another westbound train for several hours." He smiled. "I took the liberty of checking the schedule for you."

"Some chow might be nice," Longarm said. "It could be a long day ahead." He looked at Beth and raised an eyebrow. She nodded her agreement, and the two of them followed Sam Jones to a quiet café off the main street where both service and food were excellent.

"Let me," Jones said when it came time to pay. Longarm certainly had no objection to that and neither did Beth.

They had a pleasant time—Longarm thought Jones was smitten with Beth and would like to court her—then Longarm collected his carpetbag and they were at the Union Pacific depot in plenty of time to catch the westbound passenger train.

He noticed Beth surreptitiously peeking into her newly acquired coin purse while they were waiting on the platform.

"How much?" he asked her, grinning.

Beth looked a little embarrassed to have been caught counting her money, but she said, "Two hundred. It's all in gold. I've never had so much in my hand at one time, not in my whole life. It is . . . it is more than a month's salary for Hank. Mr. Jones really is a very nice man, isn't he."

"Aye, he certainly seems t' be," Longarm said, more than ever convinced that Jones would like to have more than an employer-employee relationship with Mrs. Bethlehem Bacon. He would not be at all surprised if Jones tried to get close to her should she prove to be a widow. Not that Longarm could blame the man. He would like to have some of that himself. She was an almighty attractive little bit of a thing.

Beth stood, craning her neck and peering off toward the east. "I think I see our train coming," she said.

Chapter 20

Rock Springs was raw and dusty. It was inhabited by workingmen and a few whores to service them. There were probably some fine, civilized folk who lived there, but Longarm did not happen to see any of those.

"Can we find a place where I can have a proper bath?" Beth asked.

"We'll look around," Longarm said. "There might be such."

They found a barbershop that advertised clean water in the baths, and Longarm overpaid for the privilege of Beth being the only patron. He stood outside the bathing room door to make sure she was not disturbed.

"Feel better?" he asked when she emerged, smelling strongly of soap and hot water.

"Much better, thank you. Now I have some shopping to do."

"I didn't see a ladies' wear anyplace in town," Longarm told her.

"It isn't a ladies' wear that I'm looking for," she responded. "A general mercantile should do."

"Well, there's several o' those to choose from."

They went down the street until Beth found a place she approved of, then Longarm once again stood watchfully by while she made some purchases. She bought, he noticed, men's clothing in small sizes.

"Now we need a place t' stay the night," he said when Beth had outfitted herself for riding. "Slim pickin's in that regard, but this'n over here might do."

The place was rough but the cleanest he had seen so far. The Wickiup consisted of a large building with canvas partitions dividing the interior into rooms and narrow, canvas cots in them for beds.

"Fifty cents a night, take it or leave it," the proprietor said, "and I ain't responsible for anything you leave in your room. Folks around here been known to steal, just so's you know."

"Thanks for the warning," Longarm said. "We'll take two rooms, side by side."

"All right. You can have numbers, uh, let me see . . . six and seven. The room number is painted on the wall. You won't need a key. The wall is just canvas, after all. Pull it back and go right in."

"Fine. Is there a good café close by?" Longarm asked.

"There's a café right next door." The man chuckled. "Up to you to decide if it's good or not."

They ate supper—it really was not all that bad—and returned to the rabbit warren that passed itself off as a hotel.

"I'll be right on the other side o' that drape," Longarm reminded Beth. "If you need anything, just sing out. I sleep light."

"I am sure I shall be all right, Marshal, but thank you." Beth disappeared into her cubicle and Longarm got ready for bed. The bed consisted of the hard canvas cot and one rather thin blanket. But Longarm had slept in much worse conditions. At least this night he had a roof over his head.

He lay down and quickly went to sleep.

He was awakened sometime later by a screech from the adjacent cubicle.

Chapter 21

Longarm grabbed his .45 and tumbled off the cot to the floor, banging his knee when he did so. He scrambled up and charged forward. Threw the flimsy canvas partition aside and found himself facing a swarthy man holding a knife.

The fellow was skinny and unshaven. His knife was long and slightly curved. The polished blade gleamed in the thin light coming over the partitions from a string of lanterns in the córridor beyond.

Bethlehem Bacon lay cowering on her cot, the intruder standing over her with his blade poised above her torso.

"Do it, mister, an' you die," Longarm said, straightening to his full height and cocking the Colt in his hand.

The double-action revolver was self-cocking, but Longarm had always found that the sound of oiled metal catching the sear inside the Colt was a powerful deterrent.

"Please. I'll . . . I'll give you—" Beth began.

Longarm cut her off, saying, "You'll give this son of a bitch nothing. He'll get his ugly ass outa here or he'll die right here an' now."

The man looked down at Beth and for a moment Longarm thought he was going to call Longarm's hand and plunge the dagger into her.

Then, slowly, not trusting Longarm to hold fire, he backed toward the front wall curtain.

"Stop," Longarm ordered. "Beth, d'you still have your poke? Make sure nothing's been taken before I allow this fella to step away."

She sat up and bent down to retrieve her clothes and rummage inside them. After a moment she said, "My money is gone."

Longarm motioned with the muzzle of his .45. The thief was quick to take the hint. He reached inside his coat and produced Beth's coin purse then tossed it to her.

The man started to turn away but again Longarm said, "Stop. Beth, check t' see everything's in there."

She squeezed the spring-loaded sides of the purse to pop it open, looked inside, and said, "It seems to be all right."

Longarm grunted then motioned again with his .45, this time as if shooing the intruder away. The fellow was gone in an instant.

Longarm let the hammer of his Colt back down.

"Are you okay?"

"Yes, I . . . thank you." Her breathing was rapid but she said, "I'm fine." Beth smiled. "I'm glad you were so close."

Despite the circumstances, he could not help noticing that she was wearing only the thin nightshirt. He could see the unusually small bumps in the cloth where her nipples protruded. And he could imagine the other sweet delights hidden beneath that cloth. Bethlehem Bacon was an exceptionally pretty young woman.

Beyond mere appearance, though, there was something powerfully seductive about her, as if she secreted some odor, a natural perfume, that made a man want to possess her.

Hank Bacon was one lucky son of a bitch, Longarm thought. And one very foolish man to accept work that took him away from Beth's side.

Had she belonged to Longarm, he would have wanted

to be in her bed every night. He would have wanted to fuck her every night. He wanted her now.

But she belonged to Bacon, the lucky bastard.

"I'll, uh, I'll be right here if you need me," Longarm said, backing out of Beth's room and into his own.

It was some time before Longarm was able to sleep again. His dick kept reminding him of its presence. And of Beth's, so close on the other side of the canvas wall.

Sometime during a restless night he came bolt upright on his cot, eyes wide and mouth agape.

The dagger, he thought, remembering every detail of its appearance now.

Every man he knew carried a knife. But a pocket knife, not a curved dagger like this man had in his hand.

And that hand with the dagger in it had been poised over Beth.

The son of a bitch already had her poke. There was no further need for him to be there. By all rights he should have slunk away into the night the moment he had that coin purse in hand, yet he had not done it. He was still there, poised as if to strike, when Longarm burst in on him.

The bastard had meant to kill her.

But why? Longarm chewed on that for some time before he got back to sleep again. There seemed no good reason that he could think of unless . . . unless the man was there to kill and the coin purse was only secondary. A bonus for a killer.

Longarm regretted now that he had not shot the son of a bitch. It was with that in mind that he finally drifted into a fitful sleep.

Chapter 22

Longarm woke up early, not fully rested but ready to face another day. He could hear Beth's slow, steady breathing from the other side of the canvas as she slept. He did not want to wake her so he dressed then sat on the edge of the cot, smoking an occasional cheroot, until he heard Beth begin to stir.

"Good mornin'," he said, keeping his voice low so he would not disturb anyone else.

"Good morning, Marshal. I'll be ready in just a minute. Can you wait for me?"

He smiled at that. Beth did not know it but he had been waiting for her for more than an hour already. "Yes, I can wait," he said.

He heard some scuffling and a few grunts from the other side of the wall, then Beth pulled back the partition and stepped into his room. She was grinning. It took him a moment to see why.

She was wearing her dress, as expected. But beneath it she was also wearing the trousers, men's trousers, that she had purchased the day before.

"We shall have to ride astride, I am sure," she said, smiling. "And I won't want to show my limbs. So . . ."

"Very effective," Longarm admitted.

"Can we go to breakfast now?" she asked. "I am awfully hungry."

"Sure. Let's go." He picked up his carpetbag and held aside the sheet of canvas that served as a door, motioning her ahead of him.

It was already past daybreak, and they had their choice of cafés that were open for business. Beth chose one, not too crowded, and they shared a long table with several gents.

When they were done, Beth insisted on paying for both meals. "You have been paying for everything. It's about time I pull my own weight," she said.

Longarm felt a little uncomfortable about Beth paying. He knew she had a limited amount of money and might not receive any more. Still, it was something that seemed important to her.

"Now what?" she asked as they were leaving the café.

"Now we go over to the railroad depot."

"There isn't—"

"No, there isn't a train where we're going. I want t' leave my bag with the stationmaster. It'd be awkward to take with us."

Half an hour later Longarm led the way to the BARNES AND JOHNSON LIVERY, FEED AND HAY AVAILABLE. He'd spotted the sign the day before.

The hostler gave Beth a skeptical look.

"Two saddle horses," Longarm said. "Make sure one o' them is good an' gentle."

"You can have your pick of what I got," the man responded. "Ain't none of them partic'ly gentle, though."

"Do the best you can, please. You know your animals so we'll trust your judgment," Longarm told him.

The man eyed Beth again, standing there in her dress, and said, "Don't have no sidesaddles. I got a buggy for rent, though."

"Saddle horses," Longarm said. "Two of them. And a burro for a pack animal, I think."

"Whatever you say, mister. You're the one paying the bill."

"I like that one," Beth said, pointing to a tall roan.

"That one has some spirit," the hostler said.

"He's the one I want," she insisted.

"All right, lady. It's your funeral." He stopped speaking and began to flush red in the face. "I didn't mean . . ."

"It's all right," she said. "But I do want that horse."

"Yes, ma'am."

Twenty minutes later they were ready to ride out. "We'll stop at a mercantile and provision for two weeks," Longarm said. "Then, well, then we will see what we can see up north."

Chapter 23

"Do you have any idea where we are going?" Beth asked the next afternoon. They had been riding steadily for the better part of two days and had not yet gotten out of the desert.

Longarm shrugged, not really in the mood for conversation.

"I didn't even know that Wyoming has deserts," she said, ignoring or perhaps not even noticing his lack of interest in talk.

"Now you do," Longarm said tersely. His nose was out of joint because the two of them had been thrown together night after night and Beth had gotten more and more casual about covering her body. Yet what she had was for display purposes only.

She had that magnificent ass. Cute tits. A peaches-and-cream complexion that this dry desert air was surely doing no good.

But a woman's pussy was something that could be given away as often as she liked without diminishing it or its charm.

Longarm was becoming thoroughly frustrated, to the

point that he was seriously considering whacking off. Or asking Beth to do it for him.

He wondered what her reaction would be if he asked her to jack him off. One thing was for sure—he needed some relief. He simply was not built for celibacy. He didn't know how priests did it year in and year out. Young, vigorous men, too, some of them. Probably, he thought, they pulled their own pud.

But as for him? No, thank you. Definitely not his cup of tea.

"We'll stop for the night up here," he said.

"What makes this place better than any other?" Beth asked.

"Not a damn thing," Longarm told her, "'cept we happen t' be here an' not any other place."

He pulled their little caravan to a halt and helped Beth down off the leggy roan, then stripped the saddles from the horses and the packs from the burro.

He poured some of their dwindling supply of water into his hat, watering first the horses and then the tough little burro.

"Leave that be," Longarm told Beth when she reached for the water bag to put together a pot of coffee.

"What's wrong?" she asked.

"Nothing's wrong, exactly, but we're short on water. Tomorrow sometime we ought to get into the hills. Ought t' find some live water there, maybe even a well. But we can't count on that, an' we need it more for the horses than for ourselves."

"All right, but promise me I can have a bath when we have the chance. I dream of bathing, splashing water everywhere. And drinking all I want without you glaring at me for taking too much."

"All I said was—"

"I know perfectly good and well what you said, and you were rude. You didn't have to snap at me like that."

"Huh," Longarm grunted. "It worked, didn't it?"

The day before, Beth had started to drink deeply from their supply of water, too deeply in Longarm's opinion. He had simply mentioned the fact to her. Perhaps a little forcefully. He hadn't actually shouted at her, and he really did not understand why she went on so about it.

"Tomorrow," he said.

"Lord, I do hope so. If you don't want me to make coffee, what will we drink?"

"A swallow o' water."

"That's all? One lousy swallow?"

"That's right. Just one." He managed a smile. "But you can eat all you want."

"Oh, thank you ever so much." Beth went on with her share of the camp chores, but he could tell from her stiff, jerky movements that she was thoroughly peeved.

They did not speak again for a considerable spell.

Chapter 24

"Why are you putting the fire out?" Beth complained. "It helps at least a little to keep the cold away. Besides, I like it."

"We're done cooking," he said. "Don't need a fire now. An' in flat country like this, a fire can be seen for miles around. If anybody's looking for us, this fire would tell 'em right where we are."

"Why should anyone be looking for us?" Beth asked.

"Damn if I'd know, lady, but why would that fella try to kill you back in Rock Springs?"

"Will you quit thinking such a thing? He was just a robber. You stopped him. That is all there was to that." Beth took the pins out of her hair and shook her head, sending a cascade of curls down to her shoulders.

When she reached up to remove the pins, the cloth of her bodice was pulled tight over her tits. Longarm responded with yet another hard-on. Beth either did not see or pretended not to.

Despite the rough conditions of the trail camp, she stubbornly changed into her nightshirt in the evening, shedding the dress and the rough trousers she wore underneath.

Longarm thought she looked ridiculous when she was

riding. Her legs looked normal enough, but she had her dress bunched up at her waist so she could straddle the horse.

Come evening, though, she first got out of the trousers, then when she prepared to bed down, she went through the peekaboo routine with the nightshirt and pulling her undergarments out from beneath it. Out away from town, with so little water for two humans and three animals, she could not wash out her unmentionables, but that did not stop her from taking them off at night.

And this evening she was more peek than boo, he thought. Or possibly it was only his imagination as he watched her disrobe and crawl into her bedroll.

Whatever she showed or did not show, he was plain damned horny and wanting some relief from that state of being.

He thought about saying something to her about that. Hell, she was married. She should understand how men are.

But he was interrupted by the bullet.

Chapter 25

He heard the whip-crack of it passing by and the thump as
it hit the ground somewhere off to his right, so the shooter
was to Longarm's left.

"What was . . ."

Beth started to rise. Longarm threw himself on top of
her and rolled over then over again, taking her with him,
hopefully spoiling the aim of the rifleman somewhere out
there in the darkness.

Longarm palmed his .45 and wished to hell he had
brought a rifle, too. But wishes are not fishes and cannot be
eaten. They just do not fit into a frying pan.

He lay flat on the ground and peered off in the direction
the bullet must have come from.

After a minute or so he was rewarded with the sight of a
muzzle flash and another bullet sizzled through the camp,
this time striking in the fire and sending a spray of bright
sparks high into the air.

Likely the fire had been the shooter's target, Longarm
thought. The bastard was telling them he knew right where
they were and was able to reach them.

With that in mind, Longarm grabbed Bethlehem by the

wrist and hauled her well away from the fire, out of the circle of light given off by the dying flames.

She did not protest, he noticed.

Did not protest either when he held her down, his body covering her small, warm, very shapely form.

They were being shot at. It did not matter. His hard-on was back, ragingly back. And this time Beth surely had to feel it. After all, his dick was poking her in the belly as he tried to protect her.

It was true enough that he was horny as a billy goat and thoroughly enjoyed feeling her body pressed against his. But he really was trying to protect the woman.

"All right," he said after a few minutes. "The fire's just about gone an' there ain't no light to speak of. I want you t' crawl over by the saddles an' lay down beside them. Mayhap they'll give you some protection if the son of a bitch shoots again."

"Do you think he will?" Beth's voice broke. It was obvious that she was frightened. Entirely justified, Longarm thought. Hell, he was frightened when there was somebody, he had no idea who, out there in the dark shooting at them.

"We'll wait an' find out direc'ly," he said.

They lay flat on the ground for another five minutes or so, then Longarm said, "I'm gonna leave you here while I make a scout around an' see if I can find him."

"I'm scared," Beth whispered.

"Good. You should be," he told her. "Be a damn fool not to. Now stay low. I won't be gone long."

With that, Longarm rose to a crouch and slid away into the darkness, moving as silently as he could.

Chapter 26

He knew where the rifleman had been. The muzzle flash told him that much. The point was, he knew where the man *had been*, not where he *was*. There could be a big difference. And big differences can be a problem. A fatal problem if a man is not careful.

Longarm was careful.

He took his time, moving in the general direction but not directly to the place where he'd seen the muzzle flashes.

He did not know how good this shooter was at the business of ambush and stalking, but if the man was good, he would expect Longarm to come after him and would be prepared for his position to have been seen. He would be prepared for Longarm to come for him at that place.

Consequently, if he was good, he would no longer be at that spot but would be lying nearby, ready to shoot anyone who tried to sneak up on him at the place where he'd shot from.

Longarm's task was to get out there close to where the son of a bitch must be and be even quieter than the shooter. Hunting of that sort, whether for man or game, was a matter of hearing, not seeing. It was a slow process, exhausting, nerve-wracking, requiring a maddening degree of concentration.

It took Longarm the better part of forty-five minutes to cover the seventy or eighty yards out to the spot where the shooter had been. By then he was fairly certain that the man had fired his shots and left.

Longarm found a spent .45-60 cartridge casing and a pile of horse shit. Neither gave him a clue as to who the shooter was or why he was shooting.

There had to be a reason. Neither Longarm nor Beth Bacon knew what that reason was. Or at least Beth proclaimed not to know. Longarm believed her.

He wished the woman was lying to him about that because then there would be some hope that he could get the information from her.

He slept badly that night. Likely Beth did not sleep at all. In the morning he was wary when he went to collect their animals but all three were safely where they should be.

Longarm saddled the horses and loaded their gear onto the burro.

"If I remember correctly," he told Beth, "we'll spend one more night on the ground then tomorrow we should cross the stage road. Might be we can reach a relay station there."

"Will they have water there?" she asked, returning the pins to her hair. And once again pressing the cloth of her dress tight over her tits.

Longarm nodded. "Should have."

"Enough that I can bathe?"

"That you'll have t' ask the stationmaster. It'll be up to him."

They did not speak again the rest of the morning.

Chapter 27

Late in the morning they reached a line of low, scrub-covered hills.

"Should be another ten, twelve miles to the stage road," Longarm said through lips that were beginning to crack in the dry air.

"And then?"

He only shrugged.

Beth, riding behind him, bumped her roan closer to his animal and said, "I need to stop. I'm becoming chafed."

"Did you say chaste?"

"You know perfectly well what I said. And where I meant it."

He grunted but did concede. "When we find a good spot."

"Well, you can do as you like, but I intend to stop right here. I need to get off this cursed saddle and walk around for a minute or two."

Beth's saddle rash could well have saved their lives.

From the top of a hill ahead of them a puff of white smoke blossomed and moments later a bullet sizzled past. It struck well behind and whined off into the distance.

Longarm piled off his saddle and grabbed Bethlehem around the waist, dragging her down to the ground and lying on top of her. Again. With his .45 pointed quite use-lessly in the direction the shot had come from. The range was fine for a rifle, impossibly long for a handgun.

Undeterred, Longarm cocked the Colt, took careful aim, and dusted the top of the hill where he had seen the gun smoke. If he could not hit the son of a bitch, at least he might remind him that he would not go down without a fight. He did still have a stinger.

The rifleman fired again from a different hill. And a third time from the first spot again.

He seemed a remarkably poor shot, Longarm thought. Then he looked behind and saw that the burro was down on its knees. Each of the saddle horses followed within a few minutes.

"Son of a *bitch*!" Longarm shouted.

"What . . . Marshal, what is happening?" Beth asked, her voice shaky with fear.

"We're afoot, that's what's happening," Longarm told her. "Bastard has us afoot so's he can get at us anytime he likes. An' down here away from the road, our bodies aren't likely t' be found for years. If ever."

"He's going to kill us?"

"Looks like he's gonna try," Longarm said.

"But why? What have we done that would make some-one want to kill us?"

"Little lady, I wish t' hell I could answer that question. Only thing I can think of is that it must have somethin' t' do with your husband disappearing like he done. But exactly what that'd be, I just don't know."

"I'm frightened, Marshal," she said, beginning to cry a little.

"I don't blame you." Longarm stood but no one shot at him.

"What are we going to do now?" Beth asked.

Longarm looked at her and managed a grin. "Walk," he said. "Now we walk."

Chapter 28

"What are you doing now? I thought you said we were going to walk."

"We are," Longarm told her, "but first we sit down an' eat. We won't be able t' carry so much while we're afoot, so we eat an' drink what we can from what's here. Then we load up with what we can carry an' try an' figure out how t' keep that son of a bitch out there from shooting us down like he done the horses."

Beth shot an apprehensive look toward the north where the rifle shots came from. "Is he still out there?"

Longarm nodded. "Bound t' be. But he's playing with us. Wants to stretch it out, I dunno why. Prob'ly just for fun. Bastard is havin' fun with this." He gave her a grim smile. "Up to us t' make sure he don't have any more of that kind o' fun. Now set down an' have something to eat. There's no way to have a fire without tipping that assassin to where we are an' what we're doing. Best we eat cold. I'll open some o' these cans. We won't be carrying any o' them with us anyhow. Too heavy. So enjoy some beans an' peaches now. We'll carry just water and some jerky. Anything else stays here."

Longarm used his pocket knife to open several cans

and handed them to Beth along with a spoon. He ate quickly, watchful of the hills in front of them, then opened a box of .45 cartridges and filled his pockets.

Beth watched him, her eyes wide. "Will we . . ." She stopped what she was asking and shuddered, leaving the question hanging.

Longarm picked up their half-full water bag and again smiled. "Plenty enough for the two o' us now that we don't have t' share with livestock," he said.

He lengthened the strap that held the water bag and draped it over his shoulder. "Time we move along now."

"But how will we get away from him?" Beth asked.

"He'll be expecting us t' keep going the same straight line we been traveling. What we gotta hope is that he's not watching us every minute. We got to hope he's doing something else now. Having something t' eat, tending to his horse, some damn thing—it don't matter what. Point is, we got t' hope he won't see that we aren't where he expects us t' be."

"And where will we be?" Beth asked.

"Yonder," Longarm said, pointing with his chin toward the east. "We'll take a roundabout route t' get north to that relay station. It'll take a lot longer an' mean some serious walking, but at least it gives us a chance."

He said nothing to Beth, but at the crest of a low hill to their north he thought he could see the outline of a man's hat.

The son of a bitch was indeed watching them. Longarm's detour was not fooling him. Now the question was how long the assassin intended to toy with them.

Chapter 29

"We got t' find out where the son of a bitch is," Longarm said, "so we got t' take a chance, got to trust that he wants t' keep on playing with us just a little bit longer."

"What are you trying to tell me?" Beth asked.

Longarm took a deep breath, then said, "We're gonna show ourselves to him walking north to those hills. We're gonna hope that he takes another shot or two. If he does, the smoke from his rifle will give him away." Longarm smiled. "I hope."

"And what happens if he decides he has played enough and wants to really shoot us?" she asked.

"Then all our troubles are over. The hard way," Longarm said.

Beth gave him a stricken look but said nothing for several long moments. Then she nodded, grimacing, and declared, "If I am going to die, Marshal, I am not going to do it dressed like some ragamuffin cowboy."

She hiked her dress up and unbuttoned the trousers she had been wearing while on horseback. She turned away from Longarm and slid out of the offending garment.

Longarm was treated to a look at her drawers, but

nothing more. That was enough. The woman had a genuinely lovely ass.

"There," she said, smoothing her dress. "I feel better now. At least I can die looking like a lady."

"The idea here," Longarm said, "is for us t' keep on living."

"All right. Now what?" Beth asked.

"Now we walk. First off, pointing the same way we been going. We'll let him see where he thinks we're goin'. For our part, we want t' see where he is so's we can slip away from him." Longarm gave her what he hoped was a reassuring smile. "Are you ready?"

Beth nodded, her expression grimly determined. "I am ready, Marshal."

"Then, ma'am, let's us go for a walk."

Chapter 30

The puff of white smoke and accompanying *crack* came half an hour or so later. The shooter fired from a hilltop a hundred yards or so to the left of their line of march, close enough for accurate shooting but far enough that Longarm could not charge him, far enough for Longarm's revolver to be of little use.

The bullet passed overhead and whined off to strike somewhere in the distance.

Longarm threw himself on top of Bethlehem —a far from unpleasant posture—then quickly rolled away.

"Now we crawl," he said.

"On hands and knees?"

"Exactly," he said. "On hands an' knees. From where he was shooting, he won't be able t' see us if we stay low. Follow me real close. I'll put you in a safe place."

"But—"

"Just do it, dammit," he snapped.

Moving slowly on hands and knees, he led Beth to a shallow depression where she would be out of the shooter's line of sight. He turned and laid a cautionary finger across his lips.

"Lay down an' stay still," he told her, his voice low and calm.

"Where will you—"

"I got business over there," he said, pointing toward the place where the gun smoke had been seen.

"Don't leave me alone. Please," Beth said, her eyes wide with alarm at the prospect of being left behind.

"Just do what I tell you an' everything will be all right," Longarm assured her, hoping it was true.

He made certain Beth was lying flat, then began the laborious process of stalking the son of a bitch who was shooting at them.

Longarm did not try to approach him directly. Instead he crawled at an angle toward the man, keeping brush and terrain between himself and the shooter as much as possible.

He worked his way around a hill well to the right of the shooter's last known position then rose to a crouch and palmed his .45.

After half an hour or more, he was rewarded with a glimpse of red and black checkered cloth visible beyond a clump of sage.

Longarm dropped flat and softly grunted his satisfaction.

The shooter must have realized that he'd lost sight of his intended victims. Now he was trying to find them again. And was making his way toward the spot where Longarm now lay.

Longarm waited for the man to come to him. The afternoon sun beat down on him and he wished, too late, that he had thought to remove his coat. He was thirsty and felt gritty. Beth's notion of taking a bath when they reached the stagecoach relay station was sounding more and more attractive to him. Crawling around through sagebrush and sand, knowing he could be on the receiving end of a bullet at any moment, was hard on skin, nerves, and clothing alike.

He wiped his hand free of sweat and grit then took a fresh grip on his Colt.

"Come to Papa," he whispered as the rifleman came within twenty yards of the place where Longarm lay.

The man was a complete stranger, he saw. Middle aged with dark hair, wiry and muscular in appearance. He was carrying a Spencer carbine and kept popping up high every few paces to see if he could spot Longarm and Beth, then dropping low again while he continued to move and to search.

Longarm let the fellow come a little closer, then stood and demanded, "Drop the rifle an' put your hands up. You're under arrest."

The assassin jerked, his jaw suddenly slack with surprise. "How'd you—"

He never finished the sentence. Instead he brought the Spencer up to his shoulder, pointing it in Longarm's direction.

Longarm did not wait to find out what the man might have done next. His .45 barked. And twice more.

The shooter went down with a bullet in his chest and another in his belly. Longarm did not know where his third shot went.

He hurried forward and snatched the Spencer away from the dying shooter, then knelt beside the man.

"Why're you doing this?" he asked.

But too late. The life went out of the fellow before he could have answered the question even if he had been inclined to do so.

"Shit," Longarm mumbled.

There had to be a reason these attempts were being made on him. Attempts to kill either him or Beth. He had no idea which. Or why. "Shit," he said again.

Then he stood and headed toward the spot where he had left her.

Chapter 31

"I don't . . . please, I really don't want to look," Beth protested.

"Dammit, woman, you got to. I got t' know if you recognize this man or think you know why he might be tryin' to shoot you," Longarm insisted.

Beth very reluctantly followed him back to the body of the man who had ambushed them. She stood over the corpse for some time, staring down at it, but in the end all she did was shake her head and say, "No. Sorry."

"You're sure?"

Beth turned away from the dead man and said, "I'm sure. I can't recall ever seeing this man before. I certainly don't know why he would want to shoot me. Couldn't he have been trying to shoot you instead?"

"Sure, but I ain't ever seen him before either. I was hoping you'd know something."

Longarm lifted his Stetson and wiped his forehead then looked up toward the sun. "Reckon we'd best get started. I dunno how far it is to that relay station, but we need to get there however far 'tis."

"Wouldn't this man have had a horse?" Beth asked.

"Son of a bitch," Longarm said. "You're right. I was so

worried about him that I forgot that. Let's see if can we find it."

Just after dark that evening, with Beth riding the dead man's horse—sidesaddle as she had left her trousers behind and refused to ride astride and bare her limbs to Longarm's view—light from the stagecoach relay station guided them in to baths and a hot meal.

Chapter 32

"Bacon? No, ma'am, with a name like that, I'd've been sure to remember it," the stationmaster, a man named Sam Trydon, told them. "I'm sure he never came through here."

Beth described her husband in detail, but Trydon only shook his head and repeated that he never met Hank Bacon and would surely have remembered if he ever did meet the man. "I'm sorry, lady. I wish I could help you but I can't."

Trydon smiled. "What I can help you with is something to eat. It isn't much, but it's hot and filling. Sit down, please. I'll bring you some roasted prairie chicken. It's as good as the real thing. The meat is a little darker, that's all. Mighty tasty if I do say so."

He turned and called to the dark-skinned woman who was tending the stove, "Birdy, dish up some grub for these folks."

The woman, whose hair was as sleek and shiny as a crow's wing, nodded an acknowledgment and began loading plates for the unexpected guests.

"There won't be another coach through until tomorrow afternoon. It's on its way to the reservation. Day afterward the same coach will come back, going south to Evanston.

You're welcome to wait here if you want to head back down to the railroad," Trydon said.

The woman came bearing a pair of plates with pieces of roast fowl and generous portions of fried potatoes and refried beans. The aroma coming off their meals set Longarm's belly to rumbling and his mouth to watering.

"What I want," Beth said, "is to find my husband. He won't be down at the railroad so I'll go on. To the reservation, you say?"

"Yes, ma'am. You aren't scared of Indians, are you?"

"I wouldn't know. I've never met any," Beth said.

Trydon laughed. "Not met maybe, but you've sure seen one."

"I have?"

"My woman there. She's Shoshone. Her tribe is peaceable, though. You needn't worry about them."

"Thank you, sir. Now if you will excuse me." Beth turned her attention to the supper.

Later, after she had eaten, she asked about bathing.

"Sure. We have water enough," Trydon said. He spoke to the woman in a tongue Longarm had heard spoken before but did not understand. To Beth, the man said, "She'll fix you up. The mister and me can step outside while you have your bath. Then you and Birdy can go out while the mister bathes."

Trydon looked at Longarm. "Unless you'd settle for washing yourself. You can do that at the well out back."

"A wash would do," Longarm conceded around a mouthful of prairie chicken. Once finished with his meal, he lit a cheroot and followed Trydon outside.

The two men stood smoking and admiring the heavy-bodied coach horses while Beth took that long-awaited bath.

"You just left the body laying out there?" Trydon asked at one point.

Longarm nodded. "I wasn't going to take time to bury

the son of a bitch. He didn't have anything in his pockets to tell me why he was shooting at us. Didn't have much money on him. I took what there was. I'll send it down to Denver. If we ever find out who he was, the marshal can send that money on to his kin. His horse and other traps are over there except for his rifle, I brought that inside." He gestured toward the corral, where the dead man's horse was pulling at the hay rick. "He was riding a poor sort of horse, and his saddle's been hard used. My guess is that he was hired. Hired cheap at that. But that's only a guess."

"You're a Federal marshal," Trydon said. "A man could have a grudge against you."

"Sure. It happens all the time. But this fellow . . . I never saw him before. I'm sure of that. No reason I can think of why he'd have a grudge against me."

The Indian woman appeared in the doorway and called out something in her own tongue.

"Your woman is out of the tub. We can go back in now if you like," Trydon said.

"You go ahead. I want to wash some of this grit off me. I'll be there in a few minutes," Longarm said.

"I don't know if you're a drinking man, but I have some decent bourbon in there if you like," Trydon said.

Longarm grinned. "I think that wash isn't going to take me very long. I won't be hardly a minute."

Chapter 33

"My woman there," Trydon said over the bottle of cheap whiskey, "she's a pretty good fuck. You can have her for a dollar."

"That's nice o' you. Let me think about it."

"Take your time. She ain't going nowhere and there's no other passengers staying the night." Trydon tipped the bottle back and took a healthy slug of the raw whiskey, which almost certainly was not the bourbon the label claimed it to be.

Longarm accepted the man's offer—of the whiskey, not the woman—and had another drink himself. The first drink had been fiery, the second a little raw, this third drink went down smooth and nice. "Now that's good liquor," Longarm said, almost meaning it.

"Finish it if you like. I've had enough. What did you decide about the squaw?" Trydon said.

"Maybe later."

"Oh, I get it. You're fucking the little widow woman."

"You think she's a widow?" Longarm asked.

"I'm thinking exactly the same as you are. Man disappears in this country, it usually means one thing and that's that he's dead. It happens. The Indians are mostly tame but there's bronchos among them. You know that as well as I do. Then there's bad horses that can fall and bust a man up, bad water that will twist his guts into knots, bad critters of one sort or another that can tear him apart and eat whatever's left over.

"No, this is hard country up here, Marshal, not like the soft city living down in Denver and such. My thought and I'm sure yours, too, is that the little lady is a widow." Trydon winked. "And you know what they say about widows. Once they get used to having it regular, why, there's no need to keep their legs together any longer. They come to like a good fuck as well as anyone."

"That's what they say, all right."

"Are you tapping that?" Trydon asked over the neck of the whiskey bottle.

Longarm shook his head. "Wish I was, but no, I ain't."

"Give her a little time. Once she gets used to the idea of being a widow, she'll spread 'em for you," Trydon said with a nod to affirm his own wisdom.

Longarm retrieved the bottle. The more he had of the stuff, the better it tasted. Right then it was about the finest whiskey he'd ever had. And it wasn't even rye.

"Meantime," Trydon said, "there's the Indian. Hell, for you, as good a fellow as you are, I'll knock her price down to fifty cents." He laughed. "On tick if you don't have the wherewithal on you. I know you'd be good for it."

"I'm still thinking about it," Longarm said.

"No hurry about the woman, but hand the bottle back, will you?" The stationmaster laughed again and took a drink that nearly drained the bottle. "Don't worry," he said, returning it to Longarm. "I've got more where that one came from."

When finally they staggered off to bed, Longarm's head was spinning. But that had been awfully fine whiskey. The best.

He fell asleep thinking about Bethlehem Bacon's nicely rounded ass.

Chapter 34

Longarm slept fitfully, very much aware of Beth sleeping just on the other side of a muslin partition. Trydon and the Shoshone woman had disappeared into a side room. With a wooden door, which Trydon closed. Presumably if the man could not make a dollar by peddling the woman's ass, he would fuck her himself instead.

In the morning Longarm was awake early. He sat and drank coffee with Trydon while the woman made breakfast and Beth continued to sleep.

"Got any machine oil I could borrow?" Longarm asked at one point.

"Sure thing." The stationmaster found a metal can containing a light sewing machine oil. Longarm quickly unloaded his .45 and cleaned it, then reassembled the revolver and replaced the cartridges.

"Expecting trouble?" Trydon asked.

"Not so much expecting as wantin' to be ready in case it comes," Longarm said.

Beth came out from behind the cloth room divider, her hair tousled and her eyes still sleepy. She was following the delectable aroma of frying bacon and browning biscuits. "Oh, good. Food." She sat across the table from

Longarm and asked Trydon, "When should that coach get here?"

"It varies. Likely t'will be noontime or thereabouts," Trydon said. "The passengers, if there are any, will want to have a bite to eat while me and the driver switch out the team. Then you can get aboard. Don't worry, though. You'll have plenty of notice before it pulls out." He looked at Longarm. "I'll want to be collecting the fare for you to go on. No hurry, of course. Take your time."

"Your mail contract says I ride free. So does the lady, seeing as she's a material witness in my custody," Longarm said. He noticed Beth's eyebrows go up when he said that, but she did not question him about it.

Later, though, when neither Trydon nor the Indian woman was close by, Beth leaned toward him and said, "Am I in your custody?"

He smiled. "Unless you want to pay eight dollars for the trip on to the reservation, you are."

"Oh, well if you put it that way . . ."

Beth killed time playing checkers with herself at one end of the long table—Longarm noticed that she won pretty much every time when she did that—while he found a Cheyenne newspaper that was not too old and settled down to read it from front to back, advertisements included.

He set his reading matter aside several hours later when he noticed that the Indian woman had begun cooking a large pot of prairie dog stew and guessed that meant the stagecoach was due. He had no idea how Trydon and his woman would know how many passengers to prepare for, but the two of them seemed to know their business.

The coach rolled in with a whoop and a holler and a cloud of dust not twenty minutes later.

Chapter 35

"What can I do to help?" Longarm asked as the three passengers got down from the coach and went inside the station.

"You can stay out of our way," Trydon said. "Me and Charlie know what we're doing. You try and help, you'd just get underfoot and slow us down."

"All right then," Longarm said, backing off.

He lit a cheroot and stood back to watch while Trydon and the driver unhooked the four-up from the mud wagon that was being used as a stagecoach and took the animals around back to the corrals. They returned minutes later with fresh horses in harness and expertly backed the new team into place at the front of the wagon. It took only minutes for the two men to make the exchange and have the coach ready to go again, minutes more until the passengers returned to their seats.

"Thanks, Sam," Longarm said, shaking the stationmaster's hand. "If it wouldn't offend you, I'd like t' write to your headquarters an' thank them for the help. I'll tell them you were a big help at a bad time for me."

"Good. A compliment might help get me out of this shithole and assigned someplace better. But, uh, don't mention the Indian, will you? She isn't on the payroll and it's better they don't know about her," Trydon said.

Longarm laughed. "Don't worry. I won't say a word about her." He went inside, collected Beth, and joined the other passengers in the light coach.

The coach was a refitted army ambulance with one long bench running along each side. Access was through an open doorway at the rear. The sides were open but had curtains that could be dropped to keep out rain.

Longarm felt the coach rock to the side a little when the driver climbed onto his elevated seat. That suggested the coach would roll and sway with every bump once they were moving. Passengers on such outfits had been known to get seasick from the movement, never mind that there was no sea within a thousand miles.

"See you tomorrow, Sam," Charlie called down from his driving box. Then he cracked his whip over the ears of his leaders, and the coach rocked into motion.

Longarm tugged his hat down over his eyes, folded his arms, and dropped into a light doze and a reverie that took him miles away from the moving stagecoach.

Chapter 36

It was after dark when they arrived at the White River Indian Reservation. Not that there was so very much to see there on the brightest of days. There were few buildings, and those were widely scattered. The Shoshone continued to live in teepees for the most part although a few had moved into houses.

The focal point of the reservation was the administration building and, close to it, the sutler's complex. The sutler occupied the largest structure. His building was surrounded by storage sheds, most of them little more than lean-tos. Toward the rear of the complex were two houses and a bunkhouse, where the sutler and his workers stayed.

There was also a low, sprawling hotel building with half a dozen rooms for rent.

"Come with me," Longarm told Beth, "an' keep your mouth shut. If you say anything here, that'll piss people off and we won't have a chance t' learn anything. Indians are funny that way. Women are supposed t' be quiet. Me, I been here before. I know a few of 'em, so you just set back an' let me handle things."

"I don't know what you think I might do, or say, but I assure you—"

"Shut up, Beth. Just shut up and leave be. All right?"

The woman became sullen and sulked. Longarm ignored her and led the way to the hotel.

"We need two rooms," he told the man who eventually deigned to come to the sound of a dinging bell.

The fellow dug a fingernail deep into his beard and scratched a little while he pondered the request. Finally he said, "I got one room left. You want it?"

"We want it," Longarm said.

"Where's your luggage?"

"Don't have any luggage."

"Oh. Like that, is it?"

"Mister, you are about half an inch from having your teeth shoved down your throat and your gizzard ripped out," Longarm said, his voice deceptively mild.

"One room it is, sir. It's clean. I changed the blankets just this week. That will be three dollars. In advance."

Longarm pulled out his wallet, but instead of producing the requested payment, he showed his badge. One of the requirements for being allowed to run a hotel on government land was that Federal employees were allowed to stay in the hotel free of charge.

"Well, shit," the deskman grumbled. With a sigh, he added, "Room two. Just down this hall on the right."

"Lamp?" Longarm asked.

"I can give you a candle."

"That's good enough." Longarm lit their candle then motioned for Beth to follow.

The hotel room was crude. The bed was wide enough for one. Or for two who were very friendly.

Longarm laid one of the two blankets on the floor. It would just have to do. He motioned Beth toward the bed and stretched out on the floor.

Chapter 37

The damn woman was doing it deliberately. He was halfway convinced of it. She was teasing him. Stretching his resolve almost to the breaking point.

Longarm agreed that the ride up from the relay station had been a hot and dusty experience. Of course it would be nice to sink into a cool tub.

But did she *have* to undress like that every night?

A peek here. A glimpse there. Bethlehem Bacon was putting on a better show than any Denver stripper.

What really made it maddening was that she did not seem to notice the effect she had on him.

His cock felt like an iron rod trapped inside his trousers. It should have been inside Beth's pussy. Would have been if he had his way.

And she did not even seem aware of it.

Through all their troubles, she had hung on to her nightshirt. Now she peeled off her dress and sat in her underwear while she carefully brushed the dress and hung it on a wall hook. Then she donned the nightshirt, removed her underwear—while hardly exposing a thing, dammit—and washed herself underneath the nightshirt, rinsed out the undergarments, draped them on the windowsill, and finally crawled beneath the one blanket that remained on the bunk.

Longarm would have given a month's pay to be able to crawl in next to her. On top of her. Into her. Shit, two months. Three.

No, that was an exaggeration. He had no desire to pay for pussy. But he ached to be able to fuck her.

Literally ached. His dick was so hard it was a wonder it had not popped the buttons on his fly. He could have driven nails with the damn thing.

Longarm reached down and touched himself. Slid his hand inside the waistband of his trousers and cupped his balls. Seriously considered whacking off to relieve some of the pressure.

Then he remembered a Shoshone girl he'd had the last time he was up this way.

Now there was the very model of an Indian maiden. Young and slim and pretty. And the girl fucked like a mink.

It took him a moment to pull the girl's name out of memory. Spreading Dawn, that was it. Spreading Legs would have been more appropriate.

Tomorrow, he thought. Tomorrow he would look her up and see if she still remembered how to drain a man's balls.

Longarm was smiling when he dropped off to sleep, his thoughts fixed firmly on Spreading Dawn.

Chapter 38

Longarm was up and around well before Beth stirred. He left her sleeping in the room and went to find something to eat, no small feat in a reservation headquarters that had no restaurants or cafés.

He bought some jerky from an elderly Shoshone and was sensible enough to refrain from asking just what meat it was that had been pounded, peppered, and dried. Whatever it was, it tasted fairly good.

He also walked across the compound to the headquarters building and presented himself to the agent, a newcomer since Longarm's last visit. This one was a Mormon gentleman named Thomas Payne. (No, no relation to the famous one. Different spelling, the agent explained immediately.)

"Yes, I met Hank Bacon. I remember him distinctly. Because of his name, you see. Different."

"He seems to've gone missing," Longarm said. "Hasn't been heard from in weeks."

"Now I'm sorry to hear that. He seemed a decent sort. Intelligent and nice-looking man. I liked him," Payne said. "Do you think he might have gotten himself lost? It happens, you know. You might be surprised."

"I wouldn't think so," Longarm said. "The man is a surveyor, after all. You wouldn't think a surveyor would get himself lost. Could have fallen and broken something, or a bad horse could have thrown him. Anything might happen to a man alone in the wilderness. What about your Indians? Any trouble with them lately?"

Payne shook his head. "None. The Shoshone are quiet. They haven't given any real trouble in years."

"What about the warrior societies?" Longarm asked.

"Quiet. Oh, they exist. I know that. But if they are taking any scalps, I don't hear about it. Certainly they are friendly to whites. If they did want to lift a scalp or two, it would be from a warrior in another tribe, not a white man," Payne said.

"And Bacon's horses. Were they anything special that someone, red or white, would be itching to steal?" Longarm asked.

"I don't remember anything about his horses. If he had horses. Could have had a burro or a mule for all I know."

"Thank you for your time, sir," Longarm said, extending his hand to shake.

Once on the porch outside the White River Agency, Longarm pulled out a bent and slightly frayed cheroot, his last. He dug out a match, struck it, and got the cheroot alight, then sat on a bench at the front of the building and smoked in silence while he enjoyed the morning sunshine.

When he was done with his smoke, he walked over to the rickety hotel. Beth was still sleeping.

"Are you gonna stay in bed all day?" he asked, giving her shoulder a shake.

It took her a moment to awaken and realize where she was. Then she sat up, smiling.

"Put some clothes on an' we'll go have some breakfast," he said. "I saw a fella outside selling boiled eggs. We'll want to hit him before he sells out."

"Oh. Eggs. I haven't had an egg in ever so long."

"Then get yourself dressed an' join me outside. I'll go on an' buy us some breakfast."

He left Beth in the room and went out to see what the vendor was offering. He bought eight of the small eggs. The Shoshone assured him in broken English that the eggs were fully boiled and there were no chicks inside.

When Beth came out, she looked at the little things and said, "Surely these can't be chicken eggs."

Longarm shrugged and said, "Chicken, plover, prairie hen, who knows. Point is, they're eggs. Eat them an' don't question their origin. Just consider them t' be a gift from on high."

"Did you get any salt to go on them?"

"Toughen up, woman. You can get along without salt for another day or two."

They ate in silence, but a companionable silence this time, with no tension between them.

"Will you ask about Hank at the agency?" Beth asked when they were done eating.

"Already did that. The agent remembers Hank but doesn't know what might've happened to him."

"We need to buy provisions before we go on looking," Beth said. "And horses, of course. Where can we do that?"

"We'll stock up at the sutler's across the way there, but there's some things I want t' do here at the agency before we go gallivanting off looking for him. We'll take the room for another night. I'm sure you can find something t' amuse yourself with today."

"I'm not going with you?"

"Not today," Longarm said. At that moment he was thinking about Spreading Dawn and her deep, lubricious pussy more than about Hank Bacon. "This afternoon we'll go over to the sutler's and make our purchases. You can go with me for that. You might have some special requests or something."

"All right. I'm . . . is it safe? Around these Indians, I mean? I've never been around any Indians before."

"Safe as most anyplace," he said. "As for these Indians, they're folks. Just with different ways from yours or from mine. Now if you'll excuse me, there's things I want t' do while we're here."

"Yes, of course." She yawned. "Actually I think I'm going to go get some more sleep first. This trip has been awfully tiring."

Longarm saw Beth inside, then headed for a clutch of tall, plains-style teepees, hoping to find Spreading Dawn over there or at least find someone who could tell him where her lodge was now.

Chapter 39

"Yes, I know this woman," the fat Indian lady said. She was tending a pot of something that looked terrible but smelled divine. Longarm avoided the temptation to ask what it was. He was sure his stomach would turn flip-flops of disgust if he knew.

"Where can I find her, please?"

"Oh, this woman, I don't know." She stirred the mess in the pot again using a long stick. "You got tobacco, mister?"

"No, sorry." He would gladly have paid a cigar or two for the information, but he was completely out. That was one of the many things he wanted to stock up on at the sutler's this afternoon.

This morning, however, he wanted to get laid. If only he could find Spreading Dawn.

"But I could give you a dollar. You could buy your own tobacco. Would that help?" he asked.

"Oh, I don't know."

"I really want to find Spreading Dawn," he said. "Can you help me? It's important."

"Yes. I know her. I do not know where she is now." She stirred the pot again.

"Do you know anyone who might be able to tell me?" Longarm asked.

"Yes, I know someone."

"Who?"

"You see that lodge there?" She pointed. "That woman knows this woman. You ask there, please."

Longarm sighed. He was beginning to think it might be easier to visit every lodge in the valley and look for himself than to get any information out of this woman. "Thank you."

He walked over to the lodge in question. There was another woman, also fat, squatting in front of the lodge opening. She was busy sewing something that looked like a shirt for a child.

Longarm touched the brim of his Stetson by way of a greeting and nodded. "Hello, ma'am. I'm, uh, I'm looking for a lady called Spreading Dawn. The woman over there said you might be able to help me. Can you please tell me where I can find her?"

The fat woman looked up from her needlework. "Hello, Custis."

He blinked. "Par'n?"

"I say hello to you, Custis."

The voice sounded familiar but he could not quite place it. His confusion must have showed because the fat woman began to laugh.

"What's funny?"

"You are, Custis."

"D'you know me?"

She laughed all the harder, her tits and more than ample belly rolling and heaving, her several chins quivering.

"Oh, Custis. You are so funny."

"Excuse me. I wasn't tryin' to be funny." He began to take offense to all this bullshit. "What is so damn funny about me askin' a simple question?" he demanded, his voice harsh and growing louder.

"But, Custis. You really do not know who I am, do you?"

"No, an' I would appreciate it if you could tell me where the hell I can find Spreading Dawn. You're s'posed to know where she is. So, dammit, where is she?"

"But, Custis," the sloppy fat woman said with a squeal of giggling. "It is me." She spread her hands and grinned. "I am your Spreading Dawn, Custis,"

Chapter 40

Longarm was not sure his dick would ever get over that shock and disappointment. Lordy, it had not been that long since he and a slender and lovely Spreading Dawn had snuggled up in her lodge. They had spent four nights together—or five, he could not remember for sure—and she was a wonderful fuck.

Surely it had not been *that* long.

The dumb cunt must have spent every day since that time stuffing her face. And now it looked like she had a kid, too. Not that Longarm had anything against children. Hell, he had been one himself once.

But . . . Spreading Dawn! Incredible.

That woman he'd first talked to must have been laughing, too, sending him to Spreading Dawn's lodge to ask for . . . Spreading Dawn.

But . . . Jesus. The woman was hog fat now. And ugly. He would not have believed it had he not seen it for himself.

Poor, poor Spreading Dawn.

He had pretended he looked her up to give her a present. Gave her a five-dollar gold half eagle and made like that was what he'd intended all along. He hoped she did not suspect different.

He thought rather wistfully about Bethlehem Bacon with her pert little tits and wonderfully rounded little ass. What he wouldn't have given to get into some of that!

Still, dammit, they had come here for a reason. It was about time, he thought, that he start paying attention to business and not dwelling on being so horny he was afraid he would honk.

"Washakie?" he asked at the next lodge he came to. "Where is Washakie?"

If there was anyone on the Shoshone reservation who could tell him about Hank Bacon and what had happened to the man, it should be the tribe's greatest chief.

"Where can I find Washakie?"

Chapter 41

He had trouble finding anyone who could speak English so he went back to the administration building and asked Agent Payne for some help. Payne summoned one of the young soldiers who was standing guard duty outside the agency.

"Find Adams. Tell him I need him over here," Payne ordered.

"Yes, sir."

Longarm and Payne waited on the headquarters building porch until the soldier returned. Straggling behind him was a buckskin-clad man with long, gray hair and a beard that covered his chest and a good bit of his belly.

"Whadda ya want, Tommy?"

"Deputy Marshal Custis Long, Bull Mathers. Bull is a trapper who's lived with the Shoshone for years. Married to an Indian gal. He knows the language. Bull, the marshal here needs to speak with Washakie. Would you help him out?"

"All right, but it will cost you, Tommy. I get two nights of pinochle with you."

To Longarm, Payne said, "That is the man's standard fee. He takes his pay in pinochle games. Loves to play. The pity is that he's such a terrible player."

Mathers roared. And Payne laughed. "We play at least one night a week," the agent said.

"He cheats," Mathers claimed, smiling. "I don't know how he does it, but he cheats. You want to see the chief? Come with me."

The trapper and squaw man Mathers led Longarm to a small, ordinary house set among the several buildings that made up the agency.

"This is where Washakie lives? Not in a teepee?"

"No, he wanted to live civilized. God knows why," Mathers said. Then he chuckled. "You wouldn't know it by the way he has it furnished. He turned the house into a sort of wooden teepee. Rugs and blankets and Injun stuff hanging on the walls. There's no chairs in there, just wicker seat backs. If you're invited inside—you won't be, by the way— you sit on the floor and lean against one of those things. Has a pile of furs instead of a bed. Personally I prefer a house I can pack up and move whenever the dung gets too deep." He laughed. "One way or another."

A half-dozen brown curs greeted them outside Washakie's house. Their barking announced the presence of visitors.

A small woman with gray hair and deep wrinkles met them at the door. She and Mathers exchanged some comments, then the woman went inside and Mathers motioned for Longarm to follow him onto the porch.

There were four ordinary chairs set out there. Mathers put Longarm in the one at the far end. They waited for ten minutes or so, long enough that Longarm wished he had stopped at the sutler's and bought some cigars before coming over here. Finally Washakie emerged from the house.

He did not have to be introduced. It was clear from his presence that this was a leader. There was some indefinable something about him that set the great chief of the Shoshone apart. And above.

He sat at the other end of the line of chairs and folded his arms over his chest. He and Mathers exchanged pleasantries, then after several minutes, Longarm was allowed to pose his question.

Again there was a rather lengthy exchange between Washakie and Mathers.

Mathers turned to Longarm. "Yes, he knows of Hank Bacon. Bacon let him look through, um, he doesn't have a word for it, but he means the surveyor's transit. He does not know where Bacon is now."

"Ask him if some of the young men could have robbed Bacon or killed him," Longarm said.

Mathers and Washakie spoke for a time, then Mathers said, "The chief knows that young men do foolish things, but if any of the young ones had done such a thing, he would have heard of it. This did not happen. No."

Longarm nodded. "At least I know that much now. Please thank the great chief and tell him the great white father in Washington is pleased with him."

"Yeah, I'll tell him that for sure—never mind that the great white father in Washington never heard of Washakie or anybody else out here." Mathers screwed up his mouth and spat. Longarm got a clear impression that the mountain man did not have a terribly high opinion of the folks back in Washington.

But then there were times when Longarm agreed with him about that.

Longarm thanked both Washakie and Bull Mathers and made his way back to the hotel, where Beth was napping.

Chapter 42

"I . . . I should have knocked. I'm sorry." Longarm felt his cheeks flush.

He had walked in on Beth while she was washing. She was naked, slim and beautiful and bare-assed.

She snatched up her towel as soon as the door opened but not before Longarm got a glimpse of what she kept hidden from him. He thought not for the first time that Hank Bacon was one lucky son of a bitch. And a stupid one to wander off away from Bethlehem.

If Longarm had a woman like that, she would be kept in bed twenty-three hours a day and her pussy would be permanently sore as a boil from fucking day and night.

"I'm really sorry," he said. "I just, um, don't you want t' go have some lunch?"

"Wait for me outside," she said, glaring at him, still holding the towel in front of her. Even so he could see the side of one tit, soft and pale and lovely.

He was fairly sure his hard-on was going to bust the buttons on his fly.

"Sorry," he repeated yet again and beat a hasty retreat to the front porch.

Beth took her time about finishing her bath and dressing.

When she finally did join him, she was wearing a new dress, a plain shift made of heavy linen. It was the sort of thing a warrior might buy for his squaw knowing she could decorate it to her liking with beads or shells or anything else that took her fancy.

Beth looked stunning in the simple garment. It fit her curves wonderfully well and got Longarm's dick to throbbing again.

"Can we set here an' relax for a few minutes?" he said. He did not particularly need any relaxation, but he definitely needed time for his dick to go soft again.

"Of course." She perched on a chair next to his. The dress was shorter than what white women generally wore. Her calves were bare almost to the knee. That did nothing for the state of his erection.

"You've been shopping," Longarm said, looking away from the tantalizing sight of Beth's legs.

"I bought a few things, yes."

"So I see. Learn anything?"

"Not really. You?"

He shook his head. "Not really. I need t' buy some things, too, if we're going on from here. An' we need horses and a pack animal. We got t' outfit ourselves complete."

"I have money," she said.

"So does the United States government," Longarm told her. "We'll let Uncle Sam pay this time."

"Does that mean I can buy whatever I like?"

"No, but you can get a few things that you're needin'. I don't think Uncle will mind that overmuch." He grinned. And thought about the cigars that the sutler surely would have in his store. Longarm was completely out of his cheroots. And they needed matches. Food. Everything.

He would have to sign a voucher for it all. The sutler would have to accept a government chit. His license to do business on the reservation depended on the goodwill of the Federal government, after all. You don't want to bite the hand that is feeding you.

"Ready?" he asked, rising.

"Whenever you are."

Longarm held a hand out to help Beth up, but she ignored it. He gathered that she was still angry that he'd walked in on her like that.

Chapter 43

"We had a run of trouble south o' here," Longarm explained.
"All our things was lost, so we need t' completely resupply,
right down to an' including horseflesh. Two animals t' ride
and another to pack." He showed his badge. "I'll give you a
voucher for it all."

"All right," the sutler, a man named Johnson, said. He
called, "Pierre, help this man."

Pierre was a half-breed, part French and part Ottawa.
Longarm did not know how the man was with other lan-
guages, but his English was fine.

"What you need, mister?"

Longarm smiled. "Everything."

Pierre grunted and laid out food, blankets, saddles,
hackamores rather than bridles, cooking utensils, a water
bag, ropes, tarps, and iron stakes.

"I don't s'pose you'd have a good rifle, too," Longarm
asked.

"Got trade muskets. No Sharps or Winchester, though.
You want a musket? Sixty-two caliber. Muzzle loader."

"No, thanks," Longarm said. "What about a revolver?
Cartridge only."

Pierre looked at the Colt on Longarm's belt.

"Not for me. Something for her," he said, pointing toward Beth, who was on the other side of the store looking at yard goods and sun bonnets.

"I got an Ivor Johnson thirty-eight. Breaktop. Very nice. Almost new. Be just right for the lady."

"That sounds good. And cartridges. A couple boxes for the little gun, I would think, and a couple more forty-fives for me," Longarm said.

Pierre nodded. "Boss says you want horses, too?"

"Two saddle horses and something to carry packs. Pack saddle, of course, and panniers. Those can be whatever you have. I'll want a good hatchet. And a folding saw, the best you have."

"Where you going with all this?" Pierre asked.

"North," Longarm said. "That's as close as I know. We'll be heading north from here."

Pierre grunted and went about filling their order. When it was all put together, it made an impressive pile of merchandise.

"What do you need, Mrs. Bacon?" Johnson asked, obviously wanting to fill her needs himself rather than delegate that task to Pierre.

Beth bought another linen shift, a sunbonnet, and some soft cloths. Longarm supposed those would be for her time of the month although he did not ask.

When they were done, Longarm filled out a government voucher, dated and signed it. He handed it to Johnson. "There you go, mister. Paid in full."

The sutler grunted and tucked the paper away in a cigar box along with a stack of other, similar forms he had already taken in from the agency and the soldiers at the nearby post.

Chapter 44

Longarm spent the afternoon sorting out their collection of new gear and separating it into equally balanced packs for the lop-eared mule to carry.

One of the riding animals was a mule as well. Longarm had some experience with riding mules. And liked them. Unless Beth had some objection, he would take the mule to ride and let her have the fat little pinto gelding that Pierre had found for them.

When he was satisfied with the distribution of their gear, he went back to the hotel. This time he remembered to knock before he opened the hotel room door.

"Ready for supper?"

"Oh, I already ate. Sorry," she said, obviously not sorry at all. "Were you planning on me?"

"No, just tryin' to make sure you got fed."

"I already did that," she said.

"All right then. I'll be back later sometime."

Longarm bought a chunk of stringy boiled meat—it could have been any sort of meat although Johnson claimed it was bighorn sheep—and a baked yam at the sutler's and ate them by the corral, where their horse and mules were munching hay. He was not sure but the hay might have tasted better than his meal. Still it was filling, and that was enough for the moment.

Come sundown, he began to hanker for a shot or two— or three—of whiskey. Purely medicinal, of course. Over the years he had found that a little rye whiskey was good for the stomach and helped induce sleep. Right. Medicinal.

White River being an Indian reservation, though, there was no whiskey sold here. At least none that the sutler would admit to—Longarm asked—and none that he could find elsewhere around the agency headquarters.

Eventually he gave up and returned to the hotel. Carefully knocked before entering. Beth was already in bed.

Longarm stripped down to his balbriggans and washed at the basin then stretched out on the floor with his lonely blanket.

The girl was slim with pale, pert breasts and tiny, dark-hued nipples. She had a waist no bigger than a minute and hips that flared nicely below that waist.

Her pussy hair was dark and curly. Soft to the touch and lightly scented with powder or perfume.

Her skin tasted of wood smoke and rose water. And her lips were sweet.

She smiled at him and took those lips down, kissing and licking her way down his chest and his belly. Took his swollen cock into her mouth, deep and hot, pulling at him, taking him into her throat.

Longarm cried out and pressed his face against the softness of her belly while she continued to suck him.

"Marshal Long. Wake up." Strong fingers prodded his shoulder, shaking him awake.

"Wake up, Marshal. You were talking in your sleep, and . . . I couldn't repeat the words you said. You were being quite lewd."

Longarm blinked and looked up from the floor to Bethlehem Bacon on the bed above him.

"What?"

"You were saying terrible things in your sleep. I will thank you to refrain from language like that, if you please."

Longarm scowled at the bitch and rolled over, turning his back to her. Dammit, he couldn't get laid even in his dreams while she was around.

Chapter 45

By the time the sun came up, Longarm had the animals saddled and the packs in place on the spare mule. He shook Beth out of bed, suspecting she would have stayed there half the day if he had not, and fed her a quick breakfast of jerky and canned peaches.

"Are you ready?" he inquired when the peaches were gone. If he had been alone, he would have been a half hour up the trail by now.

"Why are you in such a rush?" she demanded. "You don't even know where we are going."

"You're right. Where we're going, I never been there. But it will be easy enough t' figure out," he said.

"How in the world are you going to do that?"

"Your husband was here t' survey for a railroad, wasn't he? Well, I don't know if you've noticed but those are mountains up ahead. Trains can't climb mountains. They have t' have easy grades. So from here, we just go where we think a railroad line might be possible. That's the direction he likely would've gone."

"Oh."

Little was stirring around the agency when Longarm led them out, riding his leggy mule and leading the other.

Beth was mounted on the rather sluggish horse. Better, though, for the animal to be slow than to be so spirited that it could get away from her. Longarm figured he could handle pretty much any animal that he could strap a saddle on, but he was not so sure about Bethlehem.

They passed through the Indian encampment and moved north, Longarm leading the way and choosing the easiest grade but always seeking to move higher.

They nooned in a grove of cottonwoods above a thin trickle of snowmelt from far away and high above.

"This isn't lookin' very promising," Longarm mentioned over a cup of coffee and a piece of stick bread.

"But Hank would have come this way?"

"Likely," he said. "There's no way you an' me can know that for certain, but I'm trying t' pick the easiest rise. That's what he would've had t' do. He was thinking about rails and trains. He had t' find easy slopes or a railroad wouldn't be possible. Which, o' course, is exactly what the railroad company needed t' know."

Beth stood and looked around here. "This is such empty country. Beautiful but empty. I hate to think of Hank being up here by himself with no one to turn to for help if something bad happened."

Longarm was not thinking about Hank Bacon at that moment. He was, however, thinking about Bacon's wife. Or widow.

Beth was a lovely sight anyway, and when she turned like that, it pulled the cloth of her shirt tight against her tits, emphasizing them and the slenderness of her waist, the flare of her ass, and the length of her legs.

She had found another pair of men's trousers at the White River sutler's store and by now had completely abandoned dresses in favor of more practical clothing. A shirt and trousers did not make her look like a boy, though. She was all girl and damned pretty.

Longarm's dick agreed completely with that viewpoint.

Hank Bacon was—or had been—one fortunate son of a bitch.

He finished his coffee and wiped out the cup, then settled back and lit a cheroot to smoke while Beth finished her lunch.

"Ready?" he said when she began packing their cups back into the pack where they were stored.

"Yes. Let's go."

Four hours later Longarm drew rein and stopped on a sandy shelf just short of a thicket of chokecherry.

"Why are we stopping?" Beth asked.

"We'll camp here for the night," Longarm told her.

"So early? We still have at least two hours of daylight left."

Longarm dismounted and began to untie the packs on the mule he had been leading all day. "We want t' follow as close as possible the way your husband would've gone, right? Well, he would've been stopping every now an' then to take his survey measurements an' whatever the hell it is that surveyors do. I figure this would've been about as far as he could go that first day out from the agency. So we'll stop here, too."

Beth gave him a questioning look. But she dismounted. Took a few uncertain steps and bent backward, both hands pressing in the small of her back.

"Tired?" Longarm asked.

"Yes, of course. I suppose you are right. We should stop now."

"Why don't you set up camp? If you don't mind, I think I'm gonna take a little walk before we turn in for the night. Get my legs stretched after all day in the saddle."

"All right, but would you build the fire first? While you are doing that, I can put a pot of coffee on to boil."

He smiled. "Fine idea, thanks."

Longarm gathered wood and dry brush enough for a good fire, shaved a little tinder, and put a match to it. "There y' go. Mind you don't let it go out," he said.

"I know how to tend a fire."

"Right. Well, I'm gonna take a stroll while you handle things here."

He moved out from the camp a little distance and looked back to make sure Beth was occupying herself at the fire. Then he lengthened his stride and moved purposefully toward a patch of crackwillow a few hundred yards ahead.

The presence of magpies and buzzards ahead was the reason he had wanted Beth to stop where they did.

Something was dead up there, and Longarm wanted to see what it was before taking Bethlehem past it.

Chapter 46

It was a dry camp. Very tidy and nicely put together by someone who was accustomed to being in the wilderness. A small pot rested on flat stones next to the ashes of a fire. A sleeping bag—not blankets but an actual bag, the material stuffed with something puffy, probably feathers—was laid out next to the fire. Panniers and a pack saddle were opposite the sleeping bag.

When Longarm approached, he disturbed a feeding buzzard. The bird lumbered awkwardly into the air, a string of something moist and red trailing from its wicked beak, the sunlight glinting blue-black on its feathers.

Lace-up boots and some articles of clothing gave indication of what this bird and many others before it had been feeding on. What remained no longer appeared to be human. A good many of the bones had been torn away and gnawed. Coyotes, Longarm supposed. A bear would simply have taken the entire carcass away.

The smell at this point was of rotting meat, long overripe.

The head was fifteen feet or so away. It showed a bullet hole low in the back. A few scraps of hair clung to the dark, bloody skull, but both eye sockets were empty. Those would have been pecked out by magpies.

The murder had been coldly deliberate, the shot having been delivered while the victim was either kneeling or standing quietly in front of the killer. Longarm guessed that Hank Bacon had not known he was the target of a murderer. Possibly the surveyor assumed he was being robbed. At this point only the killer could tell the full story of what happened here.

But Longarm could see enough.

What he sorely wanted to see, but could not, was the identity of the killer who'd murdered Bacon.

Longarm spread the sleeping bag over what remained of the decomposed and half-eaten dead man and weighed it down with some rocks, hoping to keep the magpies and other carrion eaters away.

A dozen yards from the camp he noticed an iron stake driven into the ground. Curious, he walked over to it. A generous length of rope was attached to the stake and a halter lay at the other end of the rope.

Bacon had had a pack animal and had taken care of it the evening—Longarm assumed it to have been evening right after the camp was set up—shortly before he was killed.

The killer, Longarm saw, had thought to free the animal, either to steal it or to allow it to run loose. No, not to steal it. He would have kept the halter on the animal if he'd been stealing it. So he turned it loose to keep it from suffering the pangs of starvation.

Thoughtful of the son of a bitch, he was sure.

And doubly interesting now that someone was also trying to kill Bethlehem Bacon. More likely trying to have her killed. If he had been trying to do the job himself, the attempts would have stopped back there in Rawlins.

Trying to cover the fact that Hank Bacon had been murdered? Perhaps, Longarm thought.

Beth was only causing problems, looking for her husband and bringing a Federal lawman along with her when she did it. That would be reason enough for a coldhearted killer.

But who? And why? A competing railroad? That was not impossible. Improbable, perhaps, but certainly not impossible.

Longarm had many questions and no answers. The one thing he knew for sure was that now he had to go back and tell Beth that her search was over.

It was not a duty he looked forward to performing.

Chapter 47

"He didn't suffer," Longarm said. It was what one nearly always told the grieving family members but in this case it was probably true. A bullet to the back of the head meant virtually instantaneous death.

Beth stiffened her back and raised her chin. She was the one doing the suffering and was trying not to show it. "I thought he was gone," she said. "All along I thought he was gone or he would have come back to me. We were in love. He wouldn't have just disappeared."

She walked out of the firelight on the far side of the camp. Longarm could dimly see her at the edge of the circle of light. She stood there for several minutes. Composing herself, he supposed. Willing herself to accept this tragedy without showing her pain. Then she turned and came back to the fire, where he had poured himself a cup of coffee to ward off the creeping chill of the night.

"I want to see him," she said firmly.

"Not possible," Longarm told her. "It's too dark now anyway."

"In the morning then," Beth said. "I want to see my husband's body. I want to know for myself that he is gone and how it happened."

"I told you—"

"I want to see," she declared. "If you won't go with me, I'll go by myself, but I intend to see."

"Think it over tonight. See if you feel the same in the morning," Longarm said.

Beth nodded. "Very well. You will go with me?"

"I will," Longarm said.

They spoke little the rest of the evening. Beth seemed to be deep in her own thoughts, and he did not want to break in on whatever she was pondering.

He cooked their supper. Beth did not exhibit much of an appetite but she did eat a little. After supper they made an early night of it and retired to their bedrolls.

An hour or more later, judging by the swing of the stars overhead, Longarm was awakened by Bethlehem crawling into his bed.

He lay on his side and put an arm over her. She did not want sex. He understood that. What she wanted, what she needed, was simple human contact.

She lay pressed tightly against him. He could feel the heat of her tears and the trembling of her slender body as she cried.

Longarm could not help himself. He responded with a powerful hard-on. He knew good and well that Beth could feel his dick pressed against her belly. She was a married woman and would know what that was. And why. But she did not move away.

Nor did she invite anything further. She wanted to be held, wanted to be comforted, nothing more.

Once, just to be sure, he put his hand on her breast, but Beth pushed it away and stayed where she was.

Longarm held her close and let her cry it out. His erection did not go down, but he did not do anything about it.

After a while he drifted off to sleep. When he woke later to put some wood onto the fire, Beth was gone, back in her own bedroll.

Chapter 48

"You said you would go with me," Beth said, her tone one of accusation. "Instead you are squatting there cooking something. If you intend to go back on your word . . ."

"I ain't going back on nothing," Longarm told her, looking up from the skillet, where he was stirring some fried potatoes in bacon grease. "But we got things we got t' do. Including having something t' eat and packing our gear ready t' head back south when you're done over there. So don't be in a hurry. Everything over there will still be there after we've had somethin' to eat."

He dumped the potatoes onto two enamelware plates and handed one to Beth. "Here. There's salt in the bag and forks are over there."

Longarm took his own advice and moved away from the fire a little before settling down to breakfast.

When they were done eating, Longarm did the cleaning up and started packing, ready to head back.

"Aren't you ready yet?" Beth snapped, obviously irritated that he was taking so much time to pack.

"Almost done." Finally he said, "All right. Let's go."

Longarm led the way on foot to the site of Hank Bacon's last camp.

The first thing Beth did was strip the sleeping bag back so she could look at her husband's remains. She sat beside the body in silence for several minutes. When she looked up again, she said, "I don't want him buried here. I don't want him buried anywhere in this horrid country. I want to take him home with me so he can lie in the family plot."

"All right," Longarm said, "but everything considered, it's gonna take a wagon t' get him back somewhere half civilized. We can't pack the body, not in the condition it's in."

"What can we do?" she asked.

"We'll go back to the Shoshone reservation an' get someone t' come out here with a wagon an' collect the, uh, the remains. They can build a coffin that you can ship on the train east. I don't know that the stage could take such an outfit. You might have t' hire the wagon to take him all the way down to Rock Springs. D'you have money left over?"

"Enough, I think. Whatever it costs, though, I want to take him home where he belongs."

"Fair enough. We'll do what we can," Longarm assured her.

"What about his things?" Beth asked.

"There isn't all that much. Certainly nothing I think you'd want t' keep. There wasn't nothing important in his pockets. I checked them yesterday. Whoever killed him cleaned out any money he had on him."

"It was a robbery then?"

Longarm shrugged. He was not so sure that it had been, mostly because of the attempts that had been made to keep Beth from coming here.

She spent a few minutes looking around the camp. Finally she turned to Longarm and said, "What about his ledger? I see his transit is in the pack there, but what about his compass and his ledger?"

"I didn't see either o' them," Longarm said.

"Hank kept a ledger. He always did. When he was done working, after he ate he would sit and make notes and write down any readings he had taken that day. He always did that without fail. So where is his ledger now?"

"I didn't look through the packs. Could be in there," Longarm said.

"It isn't. I already looked there," Beth said.

"I can't think of a reason why a thief would think a plain ledger was important," Longarm said. "What did it look like?"

"Cloth bound in heavy canvas," she said, "much like public records books in clerks' offices but smaller, about eight by ten inches. Hank always wrote down his sightings. He made drawings and elevations and such. He never would have been without it."

"You'd think it was somewhere here then. Would a wild animal have dragged it off?"

"You tell me," Beth said. "Why would a wild creature want it?"

"Why would a two-legged creature be interested?" Longarm countered.

"Someone murdered Hank for more than the money in his pockets," Beth said.

"They did take that. Seems they took the ledger, too. Unless . . ."

Longarm stood and went over to the crude fire pit where Hank Bacon cooked his last meal. "Found it," Longarm said. "Or what's left of it."

He used a stick to stir the ashes of that last fire and dislodged several charred pieces of thick pasteboard covered on both sides by heavy gray canvas. A few partially burned pieces of bound paper remained. Someone had tried to get rid of the ledger and almost succeeded.

"Is this it?"

Beth came to him. She knelt down and picked the ledger pieces out of the ashes. "Yes. This was the ledger. I can even"—her voice choked and it took her a moment to compose herself so she could go on—"I can even see some of Hank's handwriting close to the edges here."

She collected all the pieces she could find and kept them. Longarm guessed they were her last link to her dead husband, and she intended to hang on to them.

He waited several minutes then said, "We'd best be getting on if we intend t' get back to the agency before dark."

"All right." Beth stood. But she continued to hold the pieces of Bacon's ledger. "Let's go."

Chapter 49

On the way back to the White River Agency, they spoke very little. Beth was grieving for her husband. Longarm was worrying that there was a murderer somewhere on this reservation.

"What did Hank write down in that ledger?" he asked at one point, reining his mule in so he was side by side with Beth while usually she followed to the rear of the pack mule.

"Why?" she asked.

"Because it makes no sense that someone would go to all the trouble of burning it. An' not just tossing the thing on the fire either. That wouldn't have burned it up as complete as it was. Somebody took a lot o' time with it to get it to burn so complete. There was a lot o' ash in that pit but no wood piled anywhere, and I'm betting an experienced traveler like your husband would've collected wood enough to last him through the night before he ever built his fire. Whoever killed him wanted that ledger gone, too, an' stayed there long enough t' use up all the wood that Hank would've gathered."

"I hadn't thought . . . Hank wrote down all of his elevations and compass sightings from the day, and he made copious notes. When he was done with a job, he would refer back to those notes when he was making his final report. He was very meticulous in what he put down in his ledgers, and he would keep them afterward. His office back home has a whole shelf of nothing but ledgers from past jobs so he could go back to them if he ever needed to."

Longarm grunted and said, "Thanks."

Then he was off, lost in his thoughts. He absently pulled out a cheroot, bit the twist, spat it out, then lit the slender cigar. By then he had resumed his lead position while Beth drifted back to the tail end of their tiny train.

They returned to the agency as dusk was gathering.

Chapter 50

Longarm first took care of the animals, saw Beth to their hotel room, then walked over to the agency headquarters to report Hank Bacon's death.

"Where'd you say it happened?"

Longarm told the clerk who seemed to be in charge at night.

"That's on reservation land, all right."

"Exactly," Longarm said. "It's Federal land an' a Federal crime. First thing tomorrow I want a wagon out there t' collect the remains an' any evidence they can come up with."

"Oh, I'm not sure we can do—"

"You damn well can," Longarm snapped. "I'm telling you that you can, an' I'm telling you that you're gonna do it. Do you understand me?" His voice was hard and grating as a steel file.

"Yes, sir. First light tomorrow," the clerk said. The man was soft, a little pudgy, a desk person not accustomed to action or to being spoken to like that. Probably, Longarm guessed, he was used to lording it over the Indians who inhabited the reservation.

Longarm was giving orders, not asking favors.

"I'll want the wagon, a two-horse hitch to pull it, an' a couple young men who want to make a few dollars. Make it clear we'll be gone overnight. One day there an' another day back.

"While we're out collectin' the body and the evidence, you can have a coffin made. Something sturdy. It's gotta be shipped all the way back East someplace, and I don't want it coming apart along the way."

"Yes, sir."

"Now get Bull Mathers over here. I need for him t' take me to see Washakie again."

"Yes, sir. I'll, uh, I'll do it right away."

Longarm lit a cheroot and stood there waiting while the clerk hurried to find Mathers and to make arrangements for the wagon and the young men to do the work that Longarm wanted.

The buckskin-clad mountain man joined him fifteen minutes or so later.

"Jimmy tells me you want to see Washakie again," Mathers said.

Longarm nodded. "That's right. Did he tell you why?"

"He said that surveyor's body was found. He died a natural death?"

"A bullet in the back of the head means a man is naturally gonna die," Longarm said. "Does that count?"

Mathers grunted and said, "Let's go see the chief. Maybe he's heard something though I doubt it. A bullet to the back of the head doesn't sound like one of his people."

"That's what I think, too," Longarm told him, "but I have t' ask."

"Right. Let's go."

On their way out, Longarm saw the clerk—Jimmy, Mathers had called him—making himself inconspicuous at the side of the building. Apparently Longarm intimidated the poor fellow.

Chapter 51

Longarm dragged himself back to the hotel late. He did not look at his watch but guessed the time to be ten or later. He had not taken time for supper and was ravenously hungry but even wearier after a marathon session with Bull Mathers and Chief Washakie.

There were enough rooms available this time that Longarm and Beth could each have their own, but he wanted to check on her before he slept. Or ate. Or whatever he could manage.

He knocked on her room door. She opened it almost immediately.

Beth was wearing her nightshirt, and it was obvious that she wore nothing underneath it. Her nipples poked at the cloth and made themselves known, and her tits jiggled when she walked. Horny as he was, the sight did not even elicit a hard-on.

A lamp burned on the nightstand and the bed had been turned back, but it was obvious it had not been slept in.

"Are you all right?" he asked.

"I'm fine, but you look a mess," Beth said. "Would you like to come in?"

"No need for that. I just wanted t' look in on you before I turn in."

"Let me rephrase that, Marshal. Would you please come in?"

His eyebrow went up in inquiry. "Something wrong?"

Beth hesitated, then said, "Yes. Please come in."

"Sure." He removed his hat and entered her room. There was a trunk at the foot of the bed. She must have been sitting there in order to leave the bed so undisturbed. "What's wrong, Miz Bacon?"

"Nothing." Tears began to flow from her eyes. "I miss him, Marshal."

"O' course you do. I reckon you always will. But you need t' go on anyway."

"Yes. Of course." She fabricated a smile that she obviously did not feel. "Please. Sit down. Uh, there, I suppose." She pointed toward the bed.

Longarm perched on the edge of the cot and held his hat in his lap.

"Did you see Washakie?"

"Yeah, that's where I just been."

"And did you learn anything?"

He shook his head. "Not a damn thing. The chief swears he hasn't heard anything about your husband. Mathers says I should believe him, that what Washakie doesn't hear his own self, one of his spies does. Mathers says there isn't a thing goes on anywhere on this reservation that he doesn't hear about. Mathers says he would swear your husband wasn't killed by any Indian. An' for other reasons, I feel the same."

He did not want to get into a discussion about skulls and bullet holes and what that gunshot likely meant about Hank Bacon's last moments. Beth was having a hard enough time without that.

"Then the killer will get away with it?" she said.

"I hope not, but I ain't gonna tell you anything for certain sure. All I can do is poke around an' see what comes my way. In the meantime, I've hired a wagon an' a couple young Indians. We'll drive out tomorrow to where Hank camped an', uh, collect his remains. We'll be back day after tomorrow. In the meantime they're building a stout coffin that you can take with you back home."

"You've been wonderful to me, Custis. Thank you."

He could not remember for sure but thought that might have been the first time Beth called him by his first name. He considered that to be something of a victory.

Beth came and sat beside him on the bed. Close beside him.

She reached over and placed her hand on top of his crotch. Longarm's reaction was immediate. And vigorous.

It had been too damn long since he'd had a woman, any woman, and this woman's presence had been teasing him for days.

Now he amazed himself by saying, "You're alone an' widowed an' scared. It ain't me you want but a substitute for him. So I reckon it wouldn't be a real good idea."

Longarm took her hand and moved it away from his dick. He leaned close and gave her a chaste kiss on the cheek, then stood.

"Excuse me, Beth. I'm dead tired an' want t' go to bed. But I think it'd be better for me t' do that alone tonight. When I get back with your husband's body, if you still think it's a good idea, well, we'll talk about it then."

He put his hat back on and headed for his own room.

Chapter 52

Come morning, Longarm was surprised to find Beth standing outside his room along with a young Indian, a teenager perhaps.

He tried to rub the sleep out of his eyes and almost managed it.

"Good morning," Beth said, sounding as cheerful as she had been since he'd first laid eyes on her. "I brought you some squaw bread and some slices of meat. I don't know what kind it is, but it's meat."

"Thank you. Uh, where . . ."

"I thought about it last night. I'm going with you. This is the last trip Hank will ever take, and I want to be with him," she said.

"I s'pose you should have that right," Longarm agreed. "You already know what it's like up there. If you've thought it over, then fine. What about you?" he asked, looking at the young Shoshone.

The boy just grinned, did not say a word.

"The wagon is already hitched and out front. There is another Indian boy out there, too. Did you ask them to help?"

"Yeah, I did. Figured I could use it."

"All right then. They can go on ahead. I intend to have some breakfast before we leave."

Longarm dispatched the young men with the wagon, giving them a general idea of where they should go. Once the wagon was on the way, he and Beth walked over to the sutler's to buy some boiled eggs and pickled sausages for their breakfast. After that they saddled Beth's horse and Longarm's mule and started off after the slower-moving wagon.

The boys chattered away like a pair of magpies but in their own tongue. Longarm could not understand a word they said. Not only did he understand no more than a handful of words, but they were speaking much too rapidly for him to follow even if he had had more of their language. Both seemed content, however.

Even Beth seemed in a better humor this morning.

The difference, Longarm thought, was that now she was busy. She was actively doing something toward getting Hank's body home.

They stopped to noon beside a tiny rill, ate a cold lunch, and got back on the way.

They reached Bacon's campsite late in the afternoon.

The boys seemed to have no aversion to touching Bacon's decaying remains. They piled everything they could find— body parts, bones, boots, and skull—into the dead man's sleeping bag and buttoned it closed.

Beth oversaw the operation but said little. When the boys were done and the body loaded into the light wagon, Longarm built a fire and they all settled down for the night.

Chapter 53

He was only half asleep when he heard the distinctive *crack* of a bullet flying past and the whine of a ricochet. The bullet struck, as closely as he could tell, somewhere not far to his right, which meant the shooter—he heard the rifle shot several seconds behind the bullet strike—was on the rise to his left.

Another damn gunman was after them. The rise was not a bad choice if a little too distant for this shooter's abilities. Apparently this new son of a bitch was like the one he'd already killed—someone who toyed with his victims and wanted to watch them sweat before they died.

"Down!" Longarm shouted, taking his own good advice and rolling off his bedroll and away from the ring of light cast by the fire. "Get away from the fire."

On the far side of the fire he could see that the Indian boys needed no urging. They'd already disappeared into the night.

Beth looked out from her bedroll and rose up on one elbow. She seemed sleepy and confused. "What—"

She barely had time to get the word out before Longarm threw himself on top of her and rolled away, taking her with him.

"Ouch, dammit."

"You ain't s'posed to cuss," Longarm said. "You're a lady."

"But what—"

"It's another asshole with a rifle," Longarm said.

He could feel Beth's heart thudding softly against his chest where he lay pressed tight against her. And he quickly got a hard-on that he was certain she could feel through the denim trousers she was wearing.

If she made that offer to him again . . .

But she would not. He was fairly sure of it. Dammit.

Longarm had his .45 in hand but nothing to shoot at. The rifleman was somewhere on the rise to their left, but it was a good hundred and fifty yards away and there was no way he could accurately shoot anything at that range.

"What is it?" Beth whispered.

"I don't reckon we got t' whisper," he said. "Guy has to be a hundred yards off or more. Not all that good a shot either. He needs t' be close in order to do any damage, and sweetie, I'm not gonna let him come in close. Can you lay still, I mean doin' nothing but breathing, while I take a look-see?"

"Is this just a ruse so you can feel my breast?" Beth asked.

"What? Oh. Sorry. I wasn't paying no mind to where that hand was." He chuckled. "Wish I'd noticed earlier so's I could've enjoyed it more."

He removed the offending hand and scuttled away from her.

"Stay here. Keep to the dark. I won't be long, but it will feel a lot longer than it actually is. All right?"

"Yes. All right."

Longarm holstered his .45—he would not be needing it until or unless he could get close to the rifleman—and moved silently away into the night.

Chapter 54

Longarm put on a textbook-perfect stalk on the rise where the shot had been fired. The only problem . . . there was no one there. When he finally reached the spot he was silently stalking, he stood alone in the chill night air.

"Son of a *bitch*!" he mumbled, thumb hooked into his belt only inches away from the grips of his Colt revolver.

He removed his hat and wiped the beads of sweat from his forehead then brushed off the knees of his corduroy trousers, gritty from the low profile he had kept while stalking what he thought was an ambusher.

Again, though, whoever the bastard was and whatever reason he had for trying to shoot one or both of them, he was gone now. Oh, Longarm would come back up onto the hillock in the morning and look to see if there was anything that might help him to identify the shooter. There would be nothing. He knew that. He would make the effort anyway, just in case the cocksucker slipped up and left something behind.

Cocksucker. Funny thing about that word, Longarm thought as he hiked back down to the camp, where Beth was waiting.

To call a man a cocksucker was a deadly insult that

could result in the death of one or both of the parties involved.

Yet a female cocksucker was a being to be cherished and appreciated.

When he reached the glowing embers that had been their fire, Beth was waiting for him.

"Did the boys come back?" he asked.

"Briefly. But as soon as they could, they jumped on their mules and rode away. I don't think we'll see them again unless we look them up when we get back to the agency. We, uh, we will get back to the agency, won't we?" Beth asked.

Longarm smiled reassuringly and put a hand on her shoulder. "Yeah, we'll live t' get back to the agency."

"But what about the wagon and . . . and Hank?"

"The remains are loaded on the wagon already. Come morning, we'll put my mule an' your horse into harness, and we'll drive back the same way we came up here. Before we leave, you can pick through the camp and see if there's anything else you want t' take with you. Like for a, I don't know, a keepsake," Longarm said.

"What if the man with the gun tries again to shoot us?" she asked.

"Then I'll kill the son of a bitch an' be done with it," he said, his tone flat and expression serious.

"You mean that."

"Damn right I do. Now lay down an' get some sleep. Tomorrow is gonna be a long day, and that wagon don't have any springs."

Beth returned to her bedroll but a few minutes later she sat up. "Custis?"

"Yes?"

"I hope you understand. I know you want . . . something. But I just can't. Not with Hank lying right there in the wagon. It wouldn't be right. I mean, I know, techni- cally speaking I'm a widow now and free to . . . you know.

But I wouldn't feel right about it. I owe you my life. You've protected me and taken care of me and you should be entitled to some relief, but—"

"Go t' sleep, Bethlehem. Your talkin' is keepin' me awake."

"Thank you, Custis. You're a better man than you make yourself out to be."

"Shut up, woman. I'm tired."

He heard her giggle, and after a moment she said, "Good night, Custis."

"Good night, woman."

Chapter 55

Sitting side by side on the narrow wagon seat the next day, with no one else for miles around, they had more than ample time to talk, much more than in all the days they had been together thus far.

"Hank loved these wild Western territories," Beth said. "I know he was happy on this job. He didn't believe he could find a rail route north to the mining camps, but Berriman and Jones were sure they'd make a lot of money if he could find one. Hank took the work mostly so he could come out here again. If he had to die, I'm glad it was in a place he loved so very much."

If Beth was able to talk about her husband like that, Longarm thought it was a good sign. She was accepting Hank's death.

"Can I ask you something?" he said.

"Of course. Anything." She blushed. "Well, almost anything."

Longarm laughed. He was beginning to suspect that Bethlehem Bacon was a prime catch. Her husband had been one lucky SOB. "How was Hank with strangers?"

"What do you mean?"

"Was he talkative? Did he trust people? Would he likely turn his back on someone he didn't know, for instance?"

"I know what you are really thinking when you ask those things," Beth said. "That Indian boy yesterday, Talle, Talla, Tally-something, the shorter one, he was proud of himself for the way he was taking care of Hank's skull. He brought it to show me. I saw . . . I saw the bullet hole in the back of his head, Custis.

"And no, Hank liked people well enough and could get along with pretty much anyone. But he would not have turned his back to a stranger like that."

"So you think he was killed by someone he knew?" Longarm asked. "Maybe someone he had reason to trust?"

Beth nodded, her chin firm and her eyes growing moist. "Yes, Custis. Yes, I do."

"There's another thing," Longarm said. "That ledger. I keep wonderin' why anybody would take the time to rip pages out and burn them like they done, particularly after they just murdered the man whose campfire they were using to do the burning."

"I can't answer that," Beth said, "but I know Hank's ledgers were very important to him. He was meticulous about most things but passionate about his ledgers. He started a fresh one for every job."

"So this ledger would have had his readings from this job?" Longarm said.

"Not just the numbers. He put down his thoughts, too. He put down everything that he thought might have any bearing at all on the job at hand, right down to botanical observations."

"Yet someone thought it important enough to risk . . . small risk, true, but risk nonetheless . . . staying in the camp long enough to destroy that ledger," Longarm said.

"That puzzles me, too," Beth said.

After a little while she sighed. "I suppose we will never know why they went to all that trouble instead of just discarding it. Or tossing it on the fire and letting it go at that. Instead they ripped it apart bit by bit, and that would have been no easy task. Those canvas-bound ledgers are stout."

Longarm mumbled something noncommittal, but his thoughts were churning. The killer was able to get behind Bacon. And the ledger had been important to him.

Who? Why? These were questions that needed to be answered.

There were no answers.

They rode in silence for a while after that, but a companionable silence without tension between them.

Chapter 56

They left the wagon, still containing the mortal remains of Hank Bacon, outside the sutler's complex and put their horse and mule into the corral there then walked over to the hotel, tired but satisfied that they had accomplished what was needed.

"What about supper?" Longarm asked. "There isn't a regular restaurant but we can find something at the sutler's store."

"If you don't mind, Custis, I'm really not hungry. I just want to wash and get a good night's sleep," Beth said.

He nodded. "No problem."

Longarm saw Beth safely into the hotel then helped himself to some of the jerky they had taken along with them when they went to collect the body. He ate quickly, without much interest in the food, and wished he had thought to bring a bottle of whiskey with him as he could not buy any on the reservation. It was illegal for Indians to drink alcohol in any form and illegal for anyone to sell it to them.

He settled for a long drink of water and some wistful memories to go along with it.

What this place needed, he thought, was a good, old-fashioned saloon. With dancing girls.

What it had was . . . not very damn much. With a long and heartfelt sigh, Longarm went to his room and stripped.

He hung his gun belt on a corner of the bed and treated himself to a good, all-over wash with the basin and pitcher. Feeling much better once he was clean, he stretched out on the bed and pulled the blanket over himself.

He was asleep within seconds.

Chapter 57

Longarm awoke to the squeak of the door being opened. His first thought, and first hope, was that Beth was coming to him to get what he had declined to give her before. It was an impulse he did not intend to repeat. If she wanted the comfort of feeling a dick between her legs, he was just the boy to give it to her.

He was smiling when he looked up and saw a dark figure, definitely not Bethlehem Bacon, silhouetted against the pale glow of the lamp that was burning in the hallway.

More important than the silhouette of a man, though, was the faint glint of lamplight on steel.

The intruder was holding a wicked-looking knife.

Longarm yanked his .45 out of its leather and triggered a quick shot.

He heard a grunt of shock and pain, and the would-be assassin tumbled to the floor with a bullet in his leg.

Longarm threw himself on the man and clubbed him with the butt of his .45. The fellow continued to struggle so Longarm bashed him again then wrestled the knife away from him and tossed it harmlessly to the other side of the room.

The intruder had a bullet in his leg and a bloody gash in

his scalp but he continued to buck and struggle underneath Longarm anyway.

"Hold still, dammit, or I'm gonna have to hit you again," Longarm warned.

The man continued to fight so Longarm hit him again, slamming the butt of his .45 hard against the fellow's temple. That did the job. He went limp.

Longarm sat up, breathing hard from the unexpected exertion. He fumbled in the dark for a match, struck it, and used it to light the candle that had been provided in the room.

In the faint light from the lone candle, he saw that the man who had come into the room was an Indian.

Longarm handcuffed the intruder and quickly dressed. It was not lost on him that the gunshot and sounds of a fight had not drawn any interest from other guests in the hotel. No one had come to see what the problem was. But then perhaps they were accustomed to such goings-on in the night.

By the time Longarm was dressed, the Indian was beginning to regain consciousness.

Longarm used the fellow's own sash to make a wrap around the bullet hole in his leg then dragged him to his feet.

He was not entirely sure what he should do with a prisoner on the reservation. Surely they had a jail, but he did not know where it was. He settled for hauling the Indian over to the agency headquarters.

"This'un needs to go behind bars for a spell," he said, dragging the man up the steps and into the headquarters building.

"We have a jail cell over at the army post. I can take him there if you like," the night clerk said when Longarm told him what was going on.

"Fine but first I want t' know who hired him to kill me," Longarm said, "an' why."

There was a lengthy exchange in the Indian's native tongue, then finally the clerk said, "The answer to why he came at you is simple. He was hired to do it. He would have been allowed to take your hair as a trophy, but that was just a bonus. He was paid fifty dollars in gold and promised another fifty after you were dead."

"I'm not 'specially sorry to deprive him of that second fifty," Longarm drawled, reaching for a cheroot. "Now the big question. Who hired him?"

"That he refuses to say." The clerk, a man named Jerrity, smiled. "But he is wondering if he can keep the fifty dollars he was paid up front."

Despite the circumstances, Longarm tipped his head back and laughed out loud. "Shit yes, let him keep it. But I still want t' know who's behind it."

"I wish I could tell you, but I doubt he would say even if you tortured him. Which is what he is expecting, by the way."

"Then let him an' his fifty dollars rot for a spell behind bars," Longarm said. "Can you have him taken care of from here?"

"Yes, of course."

"Then please do that. Bastard interrupted my sleep. I was right in the middle of a good dream when he woke me, an' I want t' get back to it." Longarm touched the brim of his Stetson toward the night clerk, turned, and headed back to the hotel in search of that elusive good sleep.

Chapter 58

Longarm woke up groggy and growling after a very poor night of sleep. He rubbed his chin but said the hell with shaving. That could wait a day. Or two.

He dressed slowly and checked on Beth. Her door was bolted shut. He did not try to wake her. He walked over to the sutler's complex and bought a slab of squaw bread and a can of beans for breakfast. Johnson had a pot of coffee warming on the potbelly so he helped himself to a cup.

He carried his purchases over to the side of the store and perched on a bale of dried coyote hides to enjoy his meal. While he was there, he idly watched the flow of commerce in the store.

Something he noticed almost at once was that there seemed to be two sets of prices for items—one price for the white men, mostly soldiers, who came in, the other for Indians of the Shoshone and Arapaho tribes. The Indians paid four and sometimes five times the amount that the soldiers were charged.

That was unfair. But not illegal. Johnson could charge what he damn pleased. There was no law against it.

Longarm finished eating but carried his cup over to the stove for a refill. Whatever was in the brown bean seemed to help a man wake up. And this morning Longarm needed that help. He yawned and ambled over to the counter to buy another handful of cigars, as he was getting a little low.

"Penny apiece," Pierre told him. "You got, let's see, you got seven of them there."

Longarm forked over two three-cent pieces and a penny. Pierre dropped the coins into a metal box that was kept under the counter.

"I just saw an old Indian come in and buy one cigar. You charged him a nickel. D'you know the quality of a smoke I could buy in Denver for a nickel?" he said.

"Then I suggest you buy your cigars in Denver," Pierre said, scowling.

Longarm grunted. But there was no point in getting into a pissing contest about it. He just thought it was wrong, that was all. "All right. Thanks."

"Anytime."

A young soldier wearing a red sash, which probably meant something although Longarm did not know what, came in. "Marshal Long?"

"Here," Longarm called.

The soldier presented himself and snapped to attention. "Sir, Agent Payne would like to see you. At your convenience, sir."

"All right," Longarm said, putting his coffee cup down. "Any idea what for?"

"I believe he wants you to fill out some forms, sir," the youngster said, his voice as stiff and formal as his posture.

"You can tell Agent Payne that I'll be right over there, soon as I finish my breakfast."

"Yes, sir. Thank you, sir." The soldier executed an about-face and hurried away.

Longarm picked up his coffee cup again and took it with him back to the fur bale. He was not inclined to rush anywhere just for the sake of paperwork.

Chapter 59

Once the coffee flushed the mush out of his brain, he had a third cup and then, again sitting on the bale of fur, got thinking.

These assassination attempts, or at least this last one, were directed at him, not Beth Bacon.

They were able to get two hotel rooms this time, and Beth was safe in hers with the door bolted. He knew that for a fact because he had tried her door on his way out this morning.

But the idiot with the knife had slipped into *his* room last night, not Beth's. The murder attempt was clearly directed at him.

But why?

He could understand someone giving up on trying to kill Beth once her husband's body was found. After that, if indeed keeping her from knowing about the murder was the original purpose, there was no sense in killing her.

Now the target was one United States Marshal Custis Long. Clearly.

Longarm could almost understand that. Hank Bacon's killing had taken place on Federal land and just as clearly was a Federal crime.

So someone was trying to keep the long arm of the law from snatching him up and sending him to the gallows. That made sense. So far.

The thing that really did *not* make sense to him was the burning of Hank Bacon's ledger.

Someone had hunkered down by that fire with his own murder victim lying right there beside him and taken the time to tear pages out of that heavy, canvas-bound ledger and burn them.

They'd even tried, with less success, to burn the end boards.

It took so long that they used up Bacon's entire overnight supply of firewood in the process. All of it.

Obviously this had been a long process, tearing pages out a few at a time, burning everything they could.

Now why in hell would a man go through all that?

It made no sense to Longarm.

But it most assuredly made good sense to *someone*.

Longarm bought a chunk of jerky to chew on while he sat on the fur bale and chewed on his thoughts and his confusion.

Then finally he stood, brushed himself off, and headed for the agency headquarters to see what Agent Payne had in mind this morning.

Chapter 60

"He won't be but a minute, Marshal," the day clerk, a man named Dowdell, told him.

Longarm nodded, yawned, took a seat on one of the chairs outside the agent's office. He was still chewing on the idea that he was the intended target of the assassination attempts. It really made no sense to him. He was certainly no threat to anything or anybody around this agency.

He wished he was a threat to somebody, but the sad fact was that he had no idea why he was being targeted for murder. Or by whom.

He smoked a cigar. Wished anew that he had thought to bring a bottle of whiskey with him to the dry reservation. Well, supposedly dry. Probably a man could at least buy *tizwin* here if he knew the right person to approach and the right things to say when he got there.

He made a mental note to ask Bull Mathers about that. Very likely Bull would know where a man could find a drink.

He finished the cigar. Yawned again. Looked up hopefully when Payne stepped out of his office with a sheaf of papers in his hand.

Payne, however, was not greeting Longarm but leaning over his clerk's desk.

"Dammit, Harry, they've raised the prices again. Do you know how much he is charging for a beef now? A hundred twenty dollars. Just two months ago it was an even hundred. Now he wants a twenty percent increase. Not just for the beef either. Twenty percent across the board, he says."

Dowdell took several of the papers from his boss, adjusted the spectacles that perched on the bridge of his rather large nose, and said, "It's all in order, sir. It does seem a lot to pay for one scrawny animal, but we have no choice. Not unless we want to stop issuing beef. We could, um, perhaps we could find some other source?"

"There is no other, dammit," the agent growled.

Payne looked up and noticed Longarm sitting there. "Can you believe it?" he said, grateful for this new audience to his troubles. "The prices go up practically every month. As it is, I shall have to petition the Bureau for an increase in the budget. If they don't grant the money, I don't know what we will do to feed the tribes."

"Twenty percent," Longarm said. "That seems a lot."

"Oh, it is. Believe me. Do you know how much we pay for flour? Plain, ordinary wheat flour. He charges three hundred dollars a barrel. Do you know how much the tribes consume? Especially in winter when the hunting is bad. They come in and expect to be fed. They were promised they would be fed. Promised, I tell you, by our own government. And I don't know that I can afford to feed them through the winter this year."

"Don't you have any choice?" Longarm asked, crossing his legs and leaning back in his chair.

"None," Payne said. The agent moved closer, ignoring Dowdell and giving his attention to this newcomer who would not already be familiar with his rant. "Johnson has a lock on the supply situation here. Has had since before I

was appointed to the agency. And he is charging uncon-
scionable prices for barely satisfactory goods.

"Why, you should see the cattle that he sells us. He has
them driven in twice a year, scrawny, emaciated things. The
tribes prefer to slaughter their own, you understand. We issue
beef on the hoof and they mount their ponies and chase the
poor creatures down with bows and lances and who-knows-
what. It is like hunting and they prefer it. But . . . such poor,
miserable beasts. And he charges so much for them.

"That is why I was so hopeful when that surveyor came
through." Payne turned to his clerk. "What was that man's
name again. Harry? The surveyor?"

"Hank Bacon, sir. His widow is here now to take his
body home."

"Oh, yes. Bacon. How could I have forgotten that? I had
hoped that he would bring us some bacon. And potatoes
and a thousand other things. He was here on behalf of a
railroad, you know."

"Yes, I know," Longarm said.

"Pity he was killed. That is the sort of thing that can
happen to a man traveling alone in wild country."

"That's right," Longarm said. "If, uh, if a railroad were
to come here, you would be able to buy your goods almost
at city prices, wouldn't you? Ordinary prices plus a little
for transportation."

"Exactly," Payne said with enthusiasm. "That is why I
so hoped the railroad would be coming through on its way
north."

"Right," Longarm said. "Well, sir, if you will excuse
me, there's something I have t' do."

"No, wait. I need you to fill out these arrest forms after
that incident last night."

But Payne was speaking to Longarm's back as the tall
marshal headed out the door.

Chapter 61

"Pierre!" Longarm said, entering the sutler's store and politely standing aside for a trio of young Indian women who were on their way out.

"Yes, Marshal? Did you forget something earlier?"

"More like I didn't know something earlier," Longarm told the man.

"Sorry. I don't understand," Pierre said.

"Tell me something, friend. How are you with a rifle?" Longarm asked.

"Marshal, to tell you the truth, I'm a terrible shot with any kind of gun." He laughed. "That is a large part of the reason why I became a clerk instead of a hunter or a trapper. My people are mostly trappers, but not me, as you can plainly see from this apron I'm wearing."

"But you are a very loyal employee, Pierre."

"Why, thank you, Marshal. I appreciate that."

"Is your boss in?" Longarm asked.

"He's out back taking inventory on some things. We have to order our merchandise awfully far ahead of actual need, you see, because of the time it takes to transport goods up here."

"Expensive, too, I would think," Longarm said.

"Very," Pierre agreed.

"So a railroad would make things convenient. But also much less expensive, isn't that so?"

"Perhaps. Is, uh, is there a point to all this, Marshal?"

"You know there is, Pierre. Your boss . . . and you . . . have been worried that a railroad would come along and give you competition, cut deep into your profits because of that."

"Oh, I don't know," the clerk said.

"Sure y' do," Longarm told him, his voice no longer carrying a tone of friendly banter. "Point is, so do I. I finally know what the problem has been all along. First Hank Bacon. Then his widow. An' now me. We all of us, one way or another, threatened the cozy setup you an' Johnson have had here."

"I don't know what you are talking about," Pierre insisted.

"I think you do. I think it so strongly that I'm gonna put you under arrest. We'll have t' arm wrestle to see who tries you, U.S. district court or a Shoshone tribal court. But we can work out little details like that later. Right now I want you t' turn around an' put your hands behind your back."

Instead of his hands going behind his back, Pierre reached underneath his apron.

Chapter 62

At the last second Pierre saw that he was going to be too late. He got his pistol out quickly. Longarm got his .45 even quicker.

Pierre's eyes went wide with shock and disbelief. He probably saw the puff of smoke and the lance of flame that preceded the bullet that smashed into his breastbone. He may have had time enough to realize that the marshal had just killed him. The last thing he saw in this life may well have been the dirty, mud-caked floorboards in Johnson's store.

The smoke from Longarm's gunshot boiled up between them and partially obscured Longarm's vision, but he could see well enough that Pierre had dropped his .455 Webley and fallen facedown onto the floor.

In the closed quarters the sound of the shot reverberated from the ceiling and fell like a heavy weight onto Longarm's sense of hearing. He shook his head trying to clear it and held his nose and tried to blow through it, popping his ears against the sudden pressure.

Pierre's blood flowed onto the floor. Off to the side of the big room a handful of shoppers, four Indians and a pair of off-duty soldiers, tried to make themselves look inconspicuous as they hurried out of the place.

Longarm gave the shoppers a hard look, but none of them mounted any challenge. When he was sure the store was clear except for himself and Pierre's body, he flipped open the loading gate at the back of his .45's cylinder and ejected the spent cartridge. His hearing was still impaired and he did not hear the *tink* of the empty brass hitting the floor.

He felt in his coat pocket and produced a fresh cartridge. He dropped it into the empty chamber and closed the loading gate then returned the Colt to its leather.

That cuts off the tail, he thought. Now to find the head of this particular serpent and chop that off, too.

Chapter 63

Outside the sutler's store he saw one of the soldiers who had just left the place.

"You. Corporal. Have you seen the sutler this morning?"

"Yes, sir. Just a couple minutes ago I seen him jump on a horse. Don't think it was his but he got on and started off at a larrupin' run."

"Which way'd he go?" Longarm asked.

The soldier pointed toward the northeast, a direction Longarm sincerely doubted since there was so little to be found there. Apparently the man was trying to throw him off the scent.

Longarm grunted. Paused to think for a moment. His tracking skills were good, but . . .

He headed into the village and twenty minutes later found Bull Mathers.

"I'm needin' your help, Bull." Longarm explained the situation and asked, "Can you track the man?"

"Not me, maybe, but I know someone that can. He's only a kid and an Arapaho kid at that, sixteen maybe seventeen years old, but he can track a mouse over a flat rock. He's the best I ever seen. I can get him for you if you like."

"I'd appreciate it," Longarm said.

"Wait here." Half an hour later Mathers returned with a scrawny, pimple-faced Indian boy in tow. "This is . . . Long, you wouldn't be able to pronounce his name anyhow. Just call him Hey You and you'll get along fine. But he doesn't speak any English so I'd best go along with you."

"Fine with me, Bull. Let's grab some gear and get after the man."

"He has some pals he'd like to come with us. It would be fun for them. Almost like raiding was in the old days," Mathers said.

"Fine by me. I'll get my mule and meet you in front of the headquarters building."

Longarm hurried back to the hotel and made up a pack that mostly contained cigars, matches, and jerky. He found his mule and saddled it, including breast strap and crupper, and made it back to the administration building within a quarter hour. Mathers and eight Arapaho boys, the youngest of whom could not have been more than fourteen, were already there waiting for him.

Longarm could not see any firearms among the gaggle of teenagers, but every one of them carried a lance and two of them had bows as well. They acted like they were hunting coyotes instead of a man.

Mathers spoke to Hey You and their little procession started out.

They were not two miles out of the village before Hey You said something to Mathers, who turned in his saddle and relayed the information on to Longarm.

"He says Johnson is pushing his horse too fast. He'll break the animal down if he keeps up like this."

"Tough luck for the horse," Longarm said. "Tougher for Johnson."

Late in the morning of the next day they caught up with the fleeing sutler. Johnson was walking his horse, which was limping badly on the off fore.

The Indian boys gave a whoop and rushed ahead, Longarm and Bull Mathers following at a calmer pace.

"Just hold him for me," Longarm shouted at the backsides of their racing ponies. "Me and Bull are coming."

"You realize, don't you, that they couldn't understand a word of that," Mathers said. "But don't worry. They'll get him for you."

The Indian boys raced ahead, the riders yipping and shouting, lances waving, ponies running flat out with their ears laid back.

"Shit, they're having fun, aren't they?" Longarm observed.

"This is almost like in the old days for them," Bull said. "They've never proved themselves as warriors. Too young."

"Oh, damn. What are they up to now?" Longarm said.

The boys were circling around Johnson, hollering for all they were worth. They dropped off their ponies and surrounded the sutler.

Probably, Longarm thought later, everything would have been all right except Johnson made the mistake of pulling his pistol and pointing it at one of the Arapaho.

Three lance tips lashed out, rapping Johnson's wrist and forearm. Hard. The man dropped his revolver without firing it, but by then it was too late.

Another lance thrust pierced Johnson's upper arm. Succeeding thrusts by one or more of the eight youngsters jabbed him in the kidney, the stomach, the cheek. Then the blood lust came over the boys and they punctured Johnson's gut, his balls, his throat, and finally Hey You delivered a fierce thrust into the man's heart.

By the time Longarm and Mathers reached them, Johnson was already dead and the eight newly proven warriors were painting themselves with the man's blood.

"You aren't going to arrest them, are you?" Mathers asked, sounding more than a little worried.

Longarm sighed. "The man resisted arrest. I saw that

clear enough. And no, I ain't gonna arrest them. It was a clear case o' self-defense, the way I saw it."

He reached into his pocket for a cheroot and a match, already thinking about returning to the reservation and accompanying Bethlehem Bacon back to the railroad.

There would be time along the way . . . and she was a damn fine-looking woman . . .

Longarm was smiling when he reined his mule toward the reservation and Beth.

Watch for

LONGARM AND THE MODEL PRISONER

the 436th novel in the exciting LONGARM
series from Jove

Coming in March!

GIANT-SIZED ADVENTURE FROM AVENGING ANGEL LONGARM.

BY TABOR EVANS

penguin.com/actionwesterns

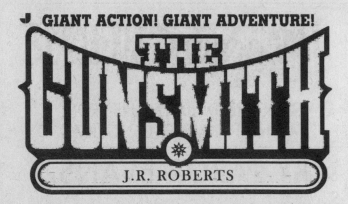

GIANT ACTION! GIANT ADVENTURE!

THE Gunsmith

J.R. ROBERTS

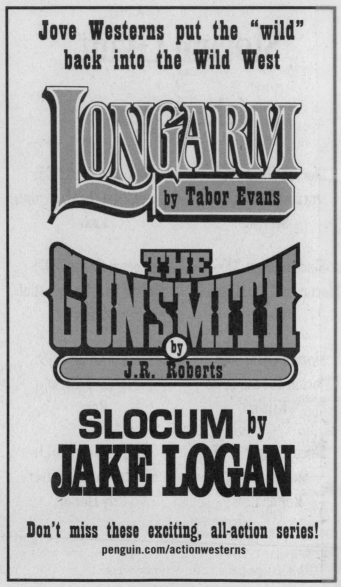